I Tell a Lie Every So Often

I Tell a Lie
Every So Often

[BY]

Bruce Clements

A Sunburst Book

Farrar, Straus and Giroux

Henry's map drawn by Bruce Clements

I am grateful to Mrs. Elizabeth Wisloh of the Eugene Smith Library of Eastern Connecticut State College, who got me materials and let me keep them a long time; to the Missouri State Historical Society, which provided microfilms; and to the Smithsonian Institution's Bureau of American Ethnology, publishers of the Thaddeus Culbertson Journal of 1850, upon which the travels in this novel are based.

TO JOYCE CAROL OATES,

WHOM I ADMIRE FOR HER

SENSE OF JUSTICE

I Tell a Lie Every So Often

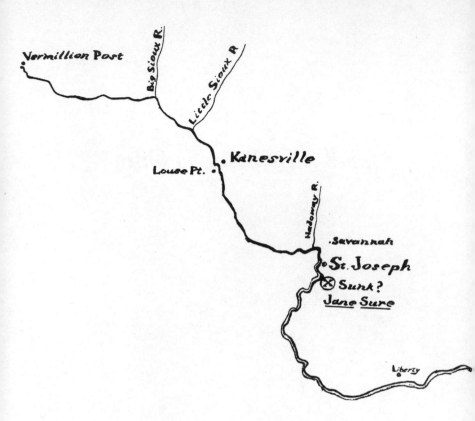

"...I travell'd hither
   through the land..."
      ~ King John, Act IV

Missouri River

Mississippi R.

⊗ Wreck of
Rowena

Travels 1848

(St Louis ～ Vermillion)

Clayton
&
Henry } Desant

St Louis

Drawn by Henry Desant

[*Chapter I*]

I TELL A LIE every so often, and almost always nothing happens, but last spring I told a lie that carried me five hundred miles and made a lot of things happen. Somebody got shot because of it, and I had a visit with a beautiful naked girl who stood up in front of me early in the morning and talked in a foreign tongue, and I saw a ball game with a hundred men on one side and a hundred men and one girl on the other side, and a boat sank, somewhat, under me, and my brother Clayton started acting strangely and sleeping with a loaded rifle, and there were some more things, too.

I was fourteen at the time all this happened, and I can't say I'm sorry about it, but I don't think I would tell the same lie again, because it could have worked out a lot worse than it did, which was in some ways bad enough. The truth is, you can never tell what's going to happen when you make up stories, or how things are going to go along once they get started.

At the time I told the lie, Miss Caroline Burke was Clayton's true heart, or at least he was courting her. Caroline has a twin sister who does not look like her or act like her at all, and this sister's name is Clytemnestra. The difference in looks is that Clytemnestra is on the shorter, fuller side, and Caroline is on the taller, thinner side. Caroline is younger than Clytemnestra, being born ten minutes after her, and she has a finer character. On the way home from church on Easter Sunday morning, April 23, 1848, Clytemnestra told us that Caroline had sewed cotton wadding into the upper part of her undergarments to make her bosom look bigger.

This news put Clayton out in a terrible way, filling up his heart with wrath, as the Bible says in different places, even though he knew that Clytemnestra Burke was always making up stories about people just for the pleasure of it. Some of her stories were funny, like the story about how the Reverend Mr. Sweetvarnish got the devil out of his cow, but most of her stories were just plain mean.

She told it to us right when we got back to her house from church. The Burkes live down the street from us on the other side, and Mrs. Burke and my mother are closer than kin. They trade back and forth being president of the Christian Ladies Alliance. One year my mother is it, and the next year Mrs. Burke is. So everybody in both families, excepting for Caroline, who was home sick with a cold in her chest, went to church that Sunday together, four Desants, that is, my mother and father and my brother Clayton and me, and the three well Burkes, that is, Mr. and Mrs. Burke and Clytemnestra, who everybody but her mother calls Clemmy, and on the way home Clayton and Clemmy and I walked together ahead of everybody else. It was a hot day, Easter last year being the closest Easter to summer in fifty-seven years, and I was in a hurry to get home and take off my church coat.

Halfway to her house Clemmy made us promise we would never tell anybody the thing that she was going to tell us, and then after we promised she acted like our promises were not sacred enough. Pretty soon we were standing in front of her house and everybody else was catching up. Then she told us the secret in a real low voice, so we had to almost climb inside of her mouth to hear, acting like she could not believe that her own twin sister would do something like that, and then right away she shrugged her shoulders, and put her finger up inside one of her curls, and said it was really a small matter, and that anyway there wasn't all that much padding. "Besides, there being diversities of gifts, I'll bet a lot of girls do it," she said, making her eyes big. "Of course, it could be the doctor prescribed for her to do it, for the sake of her illness, to keep her warm, and she'll just snip the cotton wadding out as soon as her health has fully returned. The whole world is a vanity anyway, one way and another, so why should we pay Caroline's deceit any special mind? I'm sure it does not matter to the saints and angels in heaven how big she looks, or small."

The saints and angels put aside, it mattered a lot to Clayton, but he did not know what to do. After we got home, and before dinner was ready, he just could not sit still. He kept walking back and forth, and picking up things and putting them down again, and finally he went out onto the back porch to bite his fingernails. I felt sorry for him, and I wanted to help him, even if I knew he was just making fool's trouble for himself. The worrisome thing for him was that he did not know how to find out if Caroline padded out her bosom or not. He could not just go up to her and ask her, and the only other way to find out was to marry her, and he did not want to do that until he knew the truth for sure. It was a narrow strait for him, and narrow straits are always hard on Clayton, so he was filled with mad ire and wrathful fury, as Shakespeare says in the first part of his play *King Henry the Sixth*.

"Maybe something like this you can't understand now, Henry, but some day when you're older you'll see what it means," he said, talking as if every man over seventeen always sees everything the same way, and only boys have different ideas, all of them wrong. "True or false, it's a woman's kind of deceit," he said, "and that's worse than any man's kind. What if it was the other way around? What would you feel? What if it wasn't Caroline? What if it was Clemmy that did it, and you were courting her, and you found out about it, what would you think, if it turns out to be a true fact, I mean?"

Clayton's string of questions shows that I am not the only one in the family who can fancy strange notions. Clemmy Burke, for one thing, is almost three years older than I am, and for another and worse thing, she has no heed. I'd more leave marry her dog than her, and he has got a skin disease.

"Nine chances out of ten she's lying," I said. "You know Clemmy. She doesn't care what she says."

Clayton shook his head. "It's the same thing to me,

not knowing," he said. "Besides, why should she lie about that when there are so many other better things she could lie about?"

"Like what?" I said.

"Like anything that's out in plain sight," he said.

"Maybe she has undergarments on her mind," I said. "Maybe she asked to borrow some of Caroline's, and Caroline said no, and she's trying to get her back."

"Ladies don't swap those kinds of goods," he said. "Besides which, Clemmy is naturally bigger."

Well, there was no disputing that, so instead of arguing I made him an offer. "You want me to go up in Caroline's room and see?" I asked him.

"Would you do it?" he said.

"Sure. We'll go over to her house this afternoon, and you get everybody around the piano, and I'll just run upstairs and go in her room and open her chifforobe and take a look."

"You don't let any moss grow under your feet, Henry, I'll give you that," Clayton said, and he took my hand and shook it like the Reverend Mr. Sweetvarnish does, using both of his hands and looking me right in the eye. At three o'clock sharp we went over to the Burkes' house, and as soon as Caroline came down, Clayton went over to the piano and began playing *With Holy Hope I Hark unto My Heavenly Home*, which is the loudest hymn he knows, with seven verses plus seven more in the back of the book. Even Mr. Burke, who owns a big chain forge and never says anything to anyone, opened his mouth and started singing. I crept out of the parlor at the start of the third verse, opened and shut the front door so everyone would think I had gone home or somewhere, and ran up the stairs. When I got to the second floor I looked around and saw Prince, the Burke dog, right behind me.

I went halfway down the hall so nobody could see me from downstairs, but the dog wasn't minded to follow me. He just stood there at the top of the stairs, his back sagging over a little to the left, like he might sit down, and a worried look on his face. He wasn't supposed to be upstairs, either, which he knew, and he was not sure what the right thing to do was, now that we were both up there together. He was a good dog and he wanted to do the right thing.

A lot of dogs get nervous when you look them right in the eye for long, and then they are likely to bark, especially when they're worried, so I just told him he was a good dog and turned around and went into Caroline's room. I knew where it was because I knew which way her windows looked. There was a French chifforobe with angels carved all along the front of it between her two windows, and I just stood in the middle of the room and looked at it for a while trying to decide which drawer she would be likely to keep her undergarments in.

I have to confess that I wanted to see Caroline's undergarments for myself, Clayton's needs aside. In fact, I was itching to open all six of her drawers and see everything she had. Still, I did not do it. I suppose there is something in my mind that is just dead-set against peeking. Anyway, I turned around after a minute and went back out into the hall.

They were singing Amen downstairs to one hymn, and Clayton was already starting on another. Prince stood up when he saw me, and gave a bark, but with all the noise nobody heard him. From the way he started to wag his tail you could see that barking had relieved his mind. I walked by him and went downstairs as fast as I could and back into the parlor. Clemmy was sitting on the piano bench next to Clayton singing loud and swaying back and forth. It was a slow hymn, but when he saw me Clayton started playing faster. Clayton is very musical, and he can go like the wind when he wants to. He also has a beautiful voice, and so does Clemmy.

We left as soon as we could, and when we got outside Clayton was hot for the news. "What'd you find out?" he said.

"It's just ordinary undergarments she has in there, not a bit different," I said.

"That's all?"

"Well, it's got ruffles and lace all over, but it's just like everybody else's female underclothing."

"How do you know about everybody else's?"

"You see things hanging on washlines sometimes," I said. "There's nothing special about it. It's thicker in some places and thinner in other places."

"Did you look at all of it?"

"Four suits, so it must be that Caroline is really shaped the way she looks to be."

That was the first lie, the lie that was the beginning of what happened later. It wasn't a big lie, and I only told it to make my brother feel better, and I probably would tell it again if I thought there was any need. But lies seem to come in pairs. You tell the second lie to make the first one sound better, or to get the person you told it to thinking about something else.

I could see from Clayton's face that my first lie worried him. The fact of his brother looking into his true heart's undergarments stirred him up, disquieted his spirit within him, as the Bible says. I wanted to turn his mind to something else, so I told him another lie. It was a more pure lie in one way, because it wasn't about me. Lies about yourself are always vanity, and they hardly ever sound true. I told him that the Wednesday before, while I was on my way home from the cooperage, I had met an Indian on Chouteau Street who was watching over a wagon of buffalo robes, and that we had gotten to talking, and that the Indian had told me that there was a white girl with red hair about fifteen years old living with a tribe of Indians near Fort Pierre in the Dakota Territory, and that this girl could run faster than any Indian in the tribe, man or woman.

This was a good lie to tell Clayton because nine years ago my cousin Hanna, the daughter of our Uncle John Case and Aunt Lucille, had gotten lost from off their farm near Kanesville, which is in the Council Bluffs, in Iowa. They searched for her all the way up into the Badlands but they never found her, and finally they gave her up for dead. Clayton, naturally, thought the girl I told him about might be her, and he right away saw the chance to go off into some wild country and do some great deed, like saving a captive girl in distress, who was a cousin to boot, and be a hero. My lie was the kind of lie Suffolk tells in the second part of *King Henry the Sixth*. It set out *a choir of enticing birds* for Clayton to chase after.

It was an evil lie to tell, and right after I told it I should have had the sense and goodness to confess, but I did not. It was deeper than most lies because there was a chance that it might be true, and worse because it was about somebody good. I was only five years old when Hanna got lost, or was stolen, and we were not living close to her at that time, but I remember her. Her whole family had come through Saint Louis in the spring on their way to Iowa. She was six, and she was the only one of my cousins who liked running, which was more or less the only thing I did when I was five, except for eating and sleeping. Once we ran somewhere together and hid all afternoon, but I don't remember where.

I don't have anything against my other four cousins, and I can only say good things in their favor, except that they all look like turtles, but Hanna was pretty and good and she could run like lightning. She was kind-hearted, too, so when she had to make water in the night she'd always go outside instead of using the iron chamber pot that was near the door, because it made so much noise.

On September 20, 1839, she went outside her house in the middle of the night and never came back, and nobody knows what happened to her. It could be there were some Indians around the house and they caught her. Two Indian girls had been killed by a drunk soldier in August, and she might have been taken to make up

13

for one of them. A lot of people thought she was killed and her body hidden off somewhere. Her mother and father are both dead now, and my cousin John is the head of the house and runs the farm, and nobody thinks about her.

So that was my lie, and after I had told it Clayton didn't say anything, but just kept looking at the ground. We were still out in front of the Burkes' at the time, and he started to walk home and I came along with him. He didn't say anything to me for the rest of the day.

Clayton has always been the kind of man who likes to have only one thing on his mind at a time. Now he had two things on his mind, like two scenes from different plays. One scene was me sneaking into Caroline's room, going over to her chifforobe, opening a drawer, and feeling around inside it. The other scene was Hanna walking out of her house and getting carried away by Indians into the wilderness. They were both strong scenes, no matter if they were true or false, and they stirred him up a good deal. He was like Hamlet in the play, after he talks to the ghost of his dead father who was murdered. It doesn't make any difference if the ghost is real or not. Hamlet thinks he's real, so he has to worry over what to do.

That night, right after it got dark, I climbed the tree outside of Clemmy's window, which was open because it was still hot, and threw in three small snakes. I did not do it in a spirit of spite or revenge, but only to show her that she wasn't all alone in the world to say whatever she wanted to say and make the world take her word. What she had said about Caroline was mean-spirited. Throwing the snakes was mean-spirited, too, I confess, but it was not slander.

My father is the fourth generation of our family in the coopering trade, and now I am learning it, and what with fixing barrels all day and pumping out the cellar every second night, it being a very wet spring, and reading a little each night in my book of Shakespeare, which I try to do daily to teach me what the world is like, I did not have my mind much on Indians or anything else during that next week. I did think about Clemmy every so often, because I knew she was going to send those snakes back to me one way or another, and I did not want her to take me by surprise, but my lie was pretty much not in my mind.

The first Sunday after Easter we went with the Burkes to church, everybody in both families, because by then Caroline was over her chest cold. It was a sunny day and she had on a white dress. There are some people who would say that Caroline Burke is beautiful, and that is my opinion, too, because it is a plain fact. There was a guest preacher, the Reverend Mr. John T. Otis out of the School of Divinity at Princeton, New Jersey. He was the most toward-looking man I ever saw in a pulpit. He was on his way to Saint Joseph to begin his duties as the minister of the Andrews Presbyterian Church there.

As a rule I do not like to listen to preachers, but John Otis talked sweetly and made good sense. He was not the kind to *thump you all over with words,* as Shakespeare says in *King John,* and make you wish for deafness. He preached a sermon about the frontier. In his father's time, he said, the frontier was around Saint Louis, and now it was moved all the way to California. "What was wilderness to the fathers," he kept saying, "is now home to the children, and even city." When he was done, I was sorry. Clayton paid a lot of attention to him, too, because he was waiting for the Lord to call him to be a preacher some day, and here in front of him was a man only five or six years older who had already received the call and done the book work, both. From the time he was very young, Clayton has always been certain that the Lord does not want him to make barrels.

The Burkes brought Mr. Otis to their house for supper after church, and along with him his Aunt Eusebia, a fifty-year-old lady who was going as far as Saint Joseph in his company, and then farther on by herself to the Council Bluffs to marry her second cousin, Mr. Thomas Johnson, who was in the fur trade there. The marriage had been arranged by Mr. Titus Pewbrace, a generous and kind man who is also her uncle.

I stayed with the men on the porch while the women were laying out supper inside, and I was so taken up with listening to Mr. Otis that I forgot to watch out for what Clemmy might do. I did not even think of her until I tasted the snake meat in my beef pie. She was sitting across the table from me, and I knew she was looking at me to see what I would do, so I just kept eating and listening to the talk around the table. I finished first, there being no reason for eating snake meat slowly.

I was watching Clayton more than anybody else. He put me in mind of Antony in the play *Antony and*

Cleopatra. When she gets to be too much for him, Antony leaves her and goes to Rome. "I must with haste from hence," he says, and I believe Clayton was saying the same thing to himself, more or less. It had been our plan to go to the Case farm in the middle part of June, to learn about farming and help our cousin John. At the same time, our cousin Harold was going to come from the farm to Saint Louis to learn about coopering from our father. Clayton's idea was not to wait until June, but to leave right away.

When everybody was done with dessert he cleared his throat more or less like Mr. Sweetvarnish does before he starts praying, and told Mr. Otis that he would be glad to go with him as far as Saint Joseph, and with Miss Otis all the way to the Council Bluffs, for the sake of company and protection. He had it in mind, naturally, to go on north of the Bluffs after that and hunt for our cousin Hanna. He did not ask our father's leave to make the offer, because he was just old enough not to have to.

Mr. Otis said that he would be grateful for the company if our father would permit it, and Miss Otis said about the same, and so it was agreed. The cholera season was already in full flood, and my father and mother both were glad to see Clayton leave Saint Louis as soon as convenient, and me with him.

〖 *Chapter II* 〗

FROM AFTER SUPPER until the time I went to bed I tried to settle on some answer to Clemmy Burke that she would remember and have a hard time answering back. I was almost asleep when it came to me that I should send her a disgusting poem. I read over some of Shakespeare's sonnets, and then I wrote her one using some of his rhymes and trying to sound like him. I called it *A Sonnet Poem to Clemmy Burke, Purest Angel in the World.*

> *Forsooth I fret and sweat upon my bed,*
> *Alas, I fear it is my dying hour.*
> *O look, I have a swelling in my head!*
> *And lo, my lust has made my stomach sour.*
>
> *Far far away my angel in her bed,*
> *Is sleeping like a golden lump of mud.*
> *Yet do I feel a sad and darksome dread.*
> *Dear Clytemnestra boils my oozing blood!*
>
> *Sweet Clytemnestra, Goddess of the Night!*
> *Oh flower of joy, oh raise your blazing torch,*
> *And I shall come, drawn swiftly by your light*
> *And throw up my pure passion on your porch!*

'Tis true my holy love I'll throw up soon,
And spread it all around beneath the moon!

Once I got the poem started it went fast, and I could
have written a lot more, but it was late and everybody
else was already asleep. I copied it over in brown ink
on good white paper, and put a wax seal on it, and her
name, and took it over to her house and put it in the
mailbox.

The next morning Clayton and I went down to the
river to buy passage on the *Jane Sure* as far as Saint
Joseph, which is eight days up the Missouri. The *Jane
Sure* looks like a three-floor hotel, with balconies all
around it, set on top of a flatboat. Under the hotel are
stables and storerooms, and there is a big steam engine
room in the middle. You can't tell how big it is until you
get on it, and then you think you could walk all day
and never come to the end of it.

Clayton talked to me on the way to the dock, telling
me that since he was older I was going to have to do
whatever he told me to do all the time we were traveling. "You'll just have to obey me, Henry, and that's all
there is to it," he said. I did not want to tell him I
would obey him, and I did not want to tell him I would
not obey him, so I just told him how much I would need
him to help me, which was true enough, and listened
to him talk, and in the end he didn't ask me to promise.

The spring before, when I was still in school, he
found out I was going to funerals in the afternoons,
and he gave me a long talk then, too, telling me how
young I was and how children have to listen to older

people and do what they say. I only went to funerals of immigrants who were dead of the cholera. I felt bad for them, coming all the way over from Europe, and then up the river from New Orleans, just to get sick and die in Saint Louis, and it seemed to me at the time, and it still does, that it would be at least a small comfort to the relatives to have an American around feeling bad with them. Clayton told me I had to stop going or he'd tell Father. Well, I did not say I'd stop, and I did not say I wouldn't stop, but I listened so carefully when he told me about how terrible it would be for me to die young of a disease caught from foreigners at a funeral that he didn't ask me to promise anything.

That's the way it was now. He talked for a long time about the many dangers that come to travelers in the wilderness when the younger one wants to do one thing, and the older, wiser one wants to do something else, which I'm sure is true. He talked about the savage Indians, and gave a list of the gifts of character a man needed to stay alive in the wilderness. It was a long list, with self-control, courage, strength, care, caution, steadiness, clear thinking, silence, endurance, far-sightedness, and boldness some of the things you couldn't spare. He said he wanted to make sure we kept our honor and returned from the wilderness with our flag still flying. He did not mention returning with Hanna, but surely he had that in mind, too.

By the time he was all finished we were halfway back home from the boat, and I told him I was going to try to live up to what he said, which I meant. We had bought two tickets for a room on the second floor. The tickets cost thirteen dollars each, which was about my wages for three weeks at the cooperage, but Father paid.

In the afternoon Clayton went with Father and Mr. Otis to buy some necessaries for the trip, and I was sent with Aunt Eusie Otis to help her find the way to the boat, because she had some business to do with the captain. She was the best woman, excepting my mother, that I ever met, and we were friends from that afternoon. She said what she thought, and she had passion, too.

The captain's cabin was on the top floor on the right-hand side, and there was an inside stairs that ran from it to the wheelhouse on top of the roof. The captain's name was Thomas Hanford Fountain, and when we got to his cabin he was standing at the window smoking a cigar and watching some horses get loaded on. Aunt Eusie sat down where he told her to, and he asked her what her business was, and she told him that she had come to see him about the security of her goods. "My chest is already down in the left-hand storeroom, Captain," she said, "but as we know, that is no guarantee that it will arrive safely in Saint Joseph."

"We say *port* storeroom, Miss Otis," Captain Fountain said, "and you can rest assured it will be handed over to you, safe and sound, on the dock in Saint Joseph eight or at most nine days after we depart Saint Louis."

Aunt Eusie had her hands folded in her lap and a

very friendly look on her face. "These ships sink every so often, don't they, Captain?" She was very polite when she said this.

Mr. Fountain looked at her like he was her father. "The *Jane Sure* is an excellent steamboat, Miss Otis, incorporating the latest design features. The Missouri River is high enough now for us to go far beyond Saint Joseph quite safely, were that necessary, without running aground or into snags. You need have no fear."

She smiled at him. "Did any ships go down in this river last year?"

"We call them boats, Miss Otis."

"Thank you. Do you know how many boats struck objects in the river last year, and as a result went down carrying goods and paying passengers? Ten?"

"There may have been ten."

"Could there have been as many as fifteen?"

"There could have been that many if you count them all."

Aunt Eusie smiled again. "Captain Fountain, I am planning to marry a gentleman in Kanesville, Mr. Thomas Johnson, shortly after I arrive. I am fifty years old, I have spent a number of years looking after my stepfather, who recently died, and I am looking forward to my arrival in the safe harbor of marriage, as I know you can understand. My intended is expecting to receive not only myself but a large wooden chest of my goods as well. It is a small dowry, but of some value. I have on my person a listing of its contents, if you care to look at it. I value them modestly at five hundred dollars. Do you guarantee me against their loss? Or, if not, what would be your fee to provide me with such a guarantee?"

"We do not as a rule guarantee baggage, Miss Otis. In fact, we never do."

"I see." Aunt Eusie was still as polite as can be. "Are you from Maryland, Captain?"

"Since eleven years. How did you know?"

"I have never met a Marylander who did not like to play at chances. I want to chance ten dollars with you that this boat will sink before we get to Saint Joseph. For your part, since you are sure it won't, you will want to give me favorable odds, perhaps fifty to one or forty-five to one or something of that sort. If we do not sink, you will get my ten dollars, and if we do sink, you will give me five hundred, or four hundred and fifty, depending on our agreement, and so you will save me from the mortification of having to greet my beloved without a dowry. Is that agreeable?"

"Madam, I never wager with a woman."

"And I, sir, never ascend the Missouri River, but here I am about to do it in this fine and substantial craft with its excellent captain and crew."

Captain Fountain shook his head. "Furthermore, madam, I never bet with any of my passengers."

"Then lay out the bet with a friend, some river captain who can't say no to a sure ten dollars."

The captain didn't answer, and Aunt Eusie leaned toward him. "Captain, I am an unmarried woman of small means in a world that belongs to men, and I am on my way to a safe harbor. Shall I risk arriving there with empty hands?"

The captain shook his head. "The *Jane Sure* will not sink, madam. You may accept my word on that point."

"I will wager you ten dollars it does, at fifty to one, and my friend Henry here will serve as witness."

"You don't understand, Miss Otis."

"Have you ever gone down on a boat, Captain?"

"Miss Otis, I am proud to be able to say that I don't even know how to swim."

Aunt Eusie sat back and turned her head and looked at me. "I will bet you ten dollars, Henry, that the captain regrets his ignorance in less than a week."

The captain shrugged his shoulders. "All right," he said, "if it will settle your mind, at forty-five to one, but it will have to be our secret."

"Captain, you have stepped between me and misfortune. I sincerely hope I lose my money. Now all I have to worry about is falling overboard."

Captain Fountain stood up. "Miss Otis," he said, "rest your heart. I have never once lost a member of the fairer sex. Truth to tell, you would risk a great deal more staying in Saint Louis in cholera season than you do traveling on my boat."

Aunt Eusie stood up and put out her hand. "I do not doubt the truth of that for a moment," she said, and she took his hand and shook it. Then we left and started walking home. On the way she told me about being on a boat in Lake Erie when she was twenty, and having it sink two miles from shore. "I was glad at the time to know how to swim. Not proud, only glad. My stepfather taught me. Never be proud of your ignorance, Henry. It's no gain to be ignorant of something."

That evening I went to bed early because I was tired. I had started to read the history plays, but I was so tired that I did not even open my Shakespeare book. A few minutes after one o'clock in the morning, Clayton came in my room and woke me up and made me get out from under the covers and put my bare feet on the floor to show I was awake. I could not tell at first if he was friendly or angry.

"You wrote a poem to Clemmy. Did you write a poem to Clemmy? I saw it. She showed it to me. She wouldn't let me read it, but I could see it was in your writing. That's right, isn't it?"

"It was a farewell poem," I said.

"Don't try to fool me, Henry. It was a love poem because she told me it was."

"It only sounds like a love poem because I wrote it after Shakespeare, but it isn't."

Clayton shook his head, and I could see he didn't care who I wrote it after. "Well, Henry, you made a fool of yourself writing love poems to a girl three years older than you, and you only fourteen."

By then I was awake. I could not believe what he was saying. "She thought it was a love poem?" I said.

"In red ink on white paper?" Clayton said. "What kind of poem would you think it was, if you got a poem in red ink on white paper?"

"You mean before I read it, or after?"

Clayton was very exercised. "I don't know why you think there's any use in trying to lie to me, Henry," he said. "I saw it with my own eyes."

"Well," I said, "I guess if you and Clemmy want to call it a love poem, that's what it was."

Clayton was glad to hear that. "That's what I said to you at the beginning," he said. "Put your feet under the covers or you'll catch cold. Do you think you could write another one like it? I don't mean exactly the same. A little sadder. Clemmy thought you might want to write a goodbye poem for her."

"I don't know if I could."

"I told her I'd ask you. You can please yourself, but she thought the first poem was fine. I'm bound to say that, Henry. I don't expect it takes a long time to write one, does it?"

"Not once you get started, if you feel it in your heart," I said. I was wondering when Clemmy had shown him the poem, and how it had happened, so I asked him. He did not want to tell me, but then he did. Clemmy had visited the house while I was out with Aunt Eusie in the afternoon, and given him a note telling him to meet her behind the church at ten o'clock because she had something to show him. When he got there, she let him see the paper with the poem on it, and told him about my secret love for her. They laughed at how funny it was for a while, and then all of a sudden in the moonlight they saw that they were meant to be true lovers forever, and they decided, because my poor heart was rent asunder with passion, that I should write another poem for her as a kind of medicine. Then they went back to her house, and she went inside and brought him out a true love pledge of fidelity, a belt that had kept her grandfather's pants up during the Battle of Saratoga.

By this time I was ready to start writing. I already had a pair of rhymes, *thickens* and *chickens*. He brought me paper in bed, trimmed the lantern for me, opened the window wide, told me to put my heart in it, and left. I wrote a poem called *The Love Lament of a Doomed Worm*. It was not as smooth as the first one, but finally I was satisfied. As in the first one, most of the rhymes came from Shakespeare.

A worm in love I lie upon my bed,
I crawl upon the ground, my red blood thickens.
I know that I must die, for now hath fled
My love for apples, pancakes, potatoes, and chickens.

No light remains within my fevered heart!
Just like a sad, sad, sad, sad, broken bell,
My soul is making ready to depart,
And start its long, long journey down to hell!

Oh Clytemnestra! Oh my brother Clayton!
I'm falling downward to the depths of doom!
I'll soon be dancing in the arms of Satan,
While you two dance around my bloodless tomb!

But lo, some day my soul may soon arise,
And leap to see this love poem in your eyes!

I gave it to Clayton in the morning, and he asked me to copy it over the same way I did the first. I put a wax seal on it, and he went with it to the Burkes' house.

Boats carrying goods come and go in and out of Saint Louis all day long, but most of the passenger boats go after dinner, to save the owners expense and trouble. The *Jane Sure* left after ten that night, and my mother and father and all the Burkes were on the dock waving goodbye. Just before I got on, Clemmy gave me an envelope and told me that I should not open it up until midnight, so I felt it all over to make sure there was no spider in it who could eat his way out and bite me, and then I put it in my pocket. It was a pleasure to be leaving, but it was sad to be parting from my father and mother.

⟦ *Chapter III* ⟧

THE PREACHER of our church, the Reverend Mr. Basil Arthur Sweetvarnish, is a tall man with white hair and a loud voice, and Clayton admires him more than I can say. Mr. Sweetvarnish is writing a book called *The Lord's Divine Plan for America,* and in this book he tells by chapter and verse all the things he believes God wants to have happen in this country. I know it is a big book, because every Sunday he prays out loud that God will spare him to finish the long labor of his life to His glory. Sometimes he reads part of it in his sermon.

According to the Reverend Mr. Sweetvarnish, the Americans are called by God to fill up the country and keep it pure from the Indians and the foreign unbelievers. Between the two, it's the foreign unbelievers he hates more. The Indians can't help being Indians, he says, because they are born that way, but nobody is ever born a foreign unbeliever, and all a foreign unbeliever has to do to stop being a foreign unbeliever is to go back to his own country and start believing. The Indians, he says, should all go to Mexico or Canada, and if they don't go, then whatever happens to them is the wrath of God.

Clayton is sure that Mr. Sweetvarnish is one hundred percent correct. "Indians are Indians, and Americans are Americans, and foreigners are foreigners, and it's a sin to mix them up," is what he likes to say when the talk turns that way. Seeing white men and Indians together rents up his heart entirely.

The first night, Clayton and Mr. Otis and I went to the saloon, which was at the back end of the boat next to the kitchen right underneath our room, and inside the door we saw an Indian and a white man standing up and talking French to each other. They would not sell liquor to Indians on the boat, or to anyone under recruiting age, but they let anybody into the saloon who wanted to come, and there he was, standing by the wall and talking in a high voice, almost like a girl's, and very fast. He was a big dark man, with dark brown smoky eyes, around fifty years old. When we first heard them talk, Clayton swore up and down that it was not French they were talking, and that the Frenchman, whose name I found out later was Mr. Couteaux, was an Indian. Then after we listened to them for a while, he swore up and down that the Indian was not an Indian. Finally he just walked out of the saloon and went to bed. The Indian's name was Mr. Nowac, and he was on his way back from Saint Louis to Vermillion, Iowa.

About five minutes after Clayton left, Mr. Otis left too, because he wanted to see after his aunt and write in his diary. I stayed in the saloon watching people until it was shut up, and then I went out on the deck and walked around and looked at things. There cannot be a sight in the world any prettier than the one you get when you are riding on a riverboat at night, with the black trees going by you, and the water running under-neath, which looks black except for the foam around the paddles, and the dark blue sky above you with hundreds of stars in it like pieces of clear ice, and the white moon shining down, and the boat itself, all lit up so it looks like a floating opera house.

I stayed outside for a long time looking this way and that, and it came to me that maybe, after everything was said and done, Clayton was worried about leaving home and going up into strange country. He was the one who had the gun, and having a gun makes you think of things. At least when I got one it made me think of things. So Clayton no doubt had a lot to think about that first night, which is more than likely why he forgot to tell me to go to bed. He had a short rifle, barrel and stock both, and the stock had a brass sheath around it. It was heavy, a two-hand loader, with a stiff trigger you had to pull all the way back.

The sky was getting light already when I remembered Clemmy's letter in my pocket, so I went under a lantern and opened it up. It had hearts drawn at all four corners.

Dear Henry,

I thank you kindly for the excellent poems written in my honor in recent days. Your brother esteems them equally as highly as your present correspondent, myself.

Even when you are far away from home, Henry, always do good and obey those set in authority above you as Saint Paul says, most especially your dear brother. Virtue is always remembered among the Saints and Angels in Heaven, so always abide in virtue and good deeds without ceasing. Do not trust too much in your own judgment, for you are still young and have not yet come unto a perfect knowledge of the world and its temptations.

Some day you will understand all that I have written here. Who but God can read the heart? If anything should happen to you, I forgive you all your sins against me.

Cordially,
Clytemnestra

After reading the letter, I went to bed. It was a good room we were in, no matter it being small. There were plenty of blankets, and the sound of the engine was steady and restful. It sounded like a wagon rolling across a long wooden bridge.

It was Aunt Eusie woke me up, with a bowl of the same breakfast they cooked on the boat every morning and gave out, as much as you wanted, a yellow stuff called unlyed barley that was thick and salty and didn't taste bad. They stopped giving it out at eight in the

32

morning and she wanted to make sure I had some. "We're going to have Vespers tomorrow evening," she said. "Mr. Otis is going to preach the sermon, Clayton will lead the singing, and the captain is shutting down the saloon from seven to nine. Everybody seems to carry enough whiskey with him to tide him over a dry hour, but getting the bar shut down is important." She shook the end of my bed. "Get up, slugabed," she said. "I need your services." I think she would have started to tickle my feet right then if it wasn't for the bowl of cereal on my stomach and her natural modesty about men.

She wanted me to go around the boat and tell people about the Vespers. She had a speech made up for me to recite. "Pardon me," I was supposed to say, "but you will want to know that divine services will take place on the back deck beginning at seven tomorrow evening." If anybody wanted to know more, I was supposed to tell them that Mr. Otis would be preaching, and find out if they had any favorite hymns they would like to sing.

She left then, and I got dressed and started right out. My plan was to go around the top balcony, knock on all the doors and give out my message, and then go to the saloon and get a cup of coffee, which they sold for two cents up until twelve, and then do the middle deck, and then at the end get in among the card players who were all crowded around the trestle tables at the back end of the boat outside the saloon, where everybody ate. I was just starting on the top balcony, knocking on doors and delivering my message, when we hit a snag.

The Missouri is a various river. Everything in it, rocks, stumps, trees, bars, and even holes, gets shifted around every March or April when the ice comes down, so you cannot tell when you are going to hit some kind of snag or another. Mostly the boat drags across a snag and slides off, and the worst thing that happens is a few paddle slats get broken. If the snag is big enough the boat just stops dead, like it's run into a wall, and has to drift back and go around.

When we hit this snag it sounded like every board in the boat was going to pull loose. I got slung along the balcony about fifteen feet until I hit into Mr. Nowac, the Indian, who was coming up the stairs. He asked me if I was hurt, and I told him I was not, so he let me go and walked away about his business. I thought the front of the boat might have been stove in, and we would sink, but we were lucky then and didn't.

About three or four miles farther on, we went past the *Rowena,* which was the biggest wreck on the river at the time and still is, as far as I know, unless the ice broke it up last winter. It was tipped way over to the left, and the only things you could see above water were one corner of the hurricane roof and the tops of a few windows. The man next to me at the rail said there was a cargo of mercury ore and slates on it, but the man next to him disputed the slates. The paint was still fresh and I wondered while we were going by it what kind of noise it made when the furnace got hit by the cold water.

Almost everybody on the boat played cards, but some

men played cards all the time, except when they cleared off the tables for meals. There was a man named Thomas Hesterswine playing Maine rummy. When I saw him he had been playing it all night, and he was ahead about four hundred dollars. There were three men playing with him, and some others around watching. Every time he won he'd take the money and put it in a pigskin bag on his lap. He claimed that Maine rummy was the only game he knew how to play, and that he didn't even know how to play that very well, but was just being lucky. "It's no use you asking me to play some other game," he said. "The gladdest thing I'd do in the world is quit. I don't want to play anything." Everybody was telling him he was bound to play, to give the losers a chance to win back some of their money, and there were a few men who wanted to play him because they figured his luck had to change soon. I never saw a sadder-looking man playing a game in my life, except you could see, too, that he was getting some comfort from that bag of money on his lap.

It was not until Saturday midnight, I found out later, when he had put almost nine hundred dollars in his bag, that they let him stop in honor of the Sabbath starting, but they made him promise to start in again at sundown Sunday. I was in the steam engine room a lot of the time Sunday, so I did not see him again until Sunday dinner. He did not look happy, but he ate a lot.

Sunday afternoon Aunt Eusie got a hold of a reed organ that was under shipping and started practicing on it on the front deck. It was a cold day, and windy, but she played anyway, and you could hear her almost to the other end of the boat. In the evening when it came time for the service, nearly all the passengers came. It began with Clayton leading singing, and his voice was loud enough to turn every bird shy for a mile back on both sides of the river. With him singing loud everybody else sang loud, too, and it sounded beautiful. Then Mr. Otis read the Epistle, which was from Saint Paul and told how here on earth we have no permanent place, and how all men, no matter where they are, are exiles from their true home. Then he prayed, and then he preached.

First he talked about the sadness of being away from home, like the people of Israel in Babylon or Egypt, and about how some of them stayed faithful to God, and how God watched over them and kept them for his own. He went on about this for quite a while. Mr. Hester-swine, who was sitting on a box directly in front of him, looked to have his whole heart and soul wrapped up in what Mr. Otis was saying, like he wanted the sermon to go on and on forever and never stop.

More or less halfway through his sermon Mr. Otis told my lie about Hanna, which he got from Clayton and, naturally, took to be true, which goes to show one way a lie can get spread around and made holy, as it were. She was an example, he said, of how an innocent girl stolen by savage Indians can prosper and grow strong in exile if she has the right spirit, as could be seen by the fact of her becoming a great runner, and famous among the Indians for that. He also said that she was very tall and straight, which is proof that even a clergyman, who studies more than anybody else how to discern the truth at the heart of things, can decorate a good story and not even know he is doing it.

When he started talking about Hanna, two more or less strange things happened. Mr. Nowac, who was standing up in the back, left and Mr. Hesterswine started nodding his head up and down like he knew the girl and had seen her do what Mr. Otis said she could do. He did not just nod his head a little bit and then stop, but he really made of it a testimony, so it looked like he maybe knew her, or at least that he had seen her close up.

Finally the sermon was over and everybody sang another hymn and then got up and began milling around and getting partners for cards. Five or six men went for Mr. Hesterswine, who had started talking to Mr. Otis. Of course I was curious about what he was saying, so I went over there and crowded in, too.

He was telling Mr. Otis how beautiful the preaching had been, and also how true, as he could testify from his own life. Mr. Otis answered he was glad to hear this, and thanked Mr. Hesterswine with all his heart. By now the circle of card players standing behind Mr. Hesterswine was getting bigger, but he just kept on. "I know about that girl you were telling about," he said, "and I not only know about her, I've seen her. Just last year, not far from south of the Badlands, just north of Coker's Crossing. Do you know that country?"

Mr. Otis said he didn't, and they started talking about

37

the Badlands. By this time I had worked my way around behind Mr. Otis, who was short enough to see over. "Did you talk to the girl?" I asked him.

He shook his head. "I can't talk French, or Indian either," he said.

"What does she look like?"

"Well, she dresses like an Indian," he said. "Most people take her for half Indian, half white. She's a handsome girl, not in your common way, naturally, what with all that's happened to her, and what with living outside all the while she's come around to being pretty dark-complected, but she's handsome still. Carries herself well, too, like she was all white."

"How tall is she?"

"I can't be too sure. She dresses like an Indian, I know that. I never saw her up too close, but what the Reverend Otis said about her is Gospel truth. It's a true wonder, if not a miracle, a fine girl like that living among savages and still keeping her soul, by faithfulness and the grace of God. Like the Jews in Arabia, just the same thing. God provides for his faithful children, and that right speedily, as the Gospel says. And she swims like a fish, did I tell you that?"

There was one tall card player standing directly behind Mr. Hesterswine, with his hand on Mr. Hesterswine's shoulder, but Mr. Hesterswine paid him no attention. I paid him no attention, either, I was so taken up with wondering if Mr. Hesterswine was lying or not. "How far away were you when you saw her?" I asked him.

"On the other side of the Cherry River," he said. He

started to lean forward a little, like he was getting ready to run, which he was.

"How wide is it?" I asked him.

"It's not too wide of a river for that part of the country," he said.

I was going to ask him something else, I don't remember what, but all of a sudden he slid past Mr. Otis, and as quick as a lizard he was gone. It was more or less dark by then, with only a little light coming from the moon and from the lanterns out over the front of the boat, so I couldn't see where he went. Nobody else could either. The big card player across from us just stood stock-still, with his hand hanging in the air about as high as Mr. Hesterswine's shoulder, and a surprised look on his face.

That night I woke up around midnight or later. Clayton was in his bed snoring, and there was bright moonlight coming in through the slats in the door. I decided to put on my clothes and have a cup of soup in the saloon. At home every New Year's Eve everybody gets a cup of soup at midnight and makes a wish on it for the New Year before he's drunk it up, and I thought I might make a wish for the trip.

I got the soup and took it up to the front of the boat and went in among the goods, and there I found Mr. Hesterswine. He had one leg over the side rail, and he was holding on to a post and looking down at the water going by, which looked black and cold. I said hello, and he said hello, and then for a little while we did not say anything.

"It's cold tonight," I said.

He kept looking down at the water.

"The water is more than likely cold, too," I said.

He shrugged his shoulders. "Maybe yes, maybe no."

The place we were standing was only three or four feet over the water, and I could see he was trying to make up his mind when he was going to jump in it. He had a bottle of whiskey in his free hand and was sucking on it every so often.

"You had a lot of luck at cards," I said.

He shook his head. "There was no cause for me to win that big of a pile in such a hurry. It was all their fault. They was throwing money at me hand over hand over fist."

"They say you won nine hundred dollars," I said.

He took a drink from his bottle and shook his head. "By rights that game should have lasted until almost to Saint Joseph," he said. "You see a chimney sparking up there ahead?"

I did see a chimney, but I didn't tell him I did. "It looks to me a long way to shore," I said.

He squinted his eyes and pushed out his lips. "Not so long. Here's what I want you to do, and I'll give you ten dollars gold for it. You tell it around among the passengers tomorrow morning that you just came from my room, 216 on the top balcony, left side, and that I gave you ten cents to bring me my breakfast, and that you did it."

I shook my head. "I don't think I want to say that, thank you all the same," I said.

My father told me once never to kiss another man's hog for money, and that was more or less what Mr.

Hesterswine was asking me to do. Telling a lie for pleasure is less of a crime, it seems to me, than telling a lie for pay. There is no dignity in that at all.

We were coming up to the house, which was set up on a little bluff right over the riverbank, almost close enough to reach with a stone. Mr. Hesterswine pulled his other leg over the rail and knelt down and hopped into the water. He said "Oh" when he hit, and then he started swimming. I tried to watch him to see if he got to shore, but it was too dark and we were moving away from him. I didn't worry about him, though. He was thin, but he looked strong, and he was not too drunk to swim forty yards.

My soup was cold already, but I stayed where I was, drinking it and wondering what would happen if my lie turned out to be true. I thought about Hanna, fifteen years old and living with the Indians, and I wondered what I would do if I was her and Clayton came crawling into my tepee late one night and shook me awake and told me that he was my cousin who had come to rescue me and bring me back to the farm. Would I remember enough English to understand what he was saying to me, and if I did, would I get up and run away with him? Would I want to be white after nine years of being Indian?

I kept thinking about these matters until the wind started blowing hard, and then I went back to bed. I never did make a wish on my soup.

Not much happened for the rest of the trip, and then a few miles from Saint Joseph we sank, more or less. Most of the time before that I spent either playing long card games with Aunt Eusie or sitting in the front of the boat looking at the country and reading the history plays in my Shakespeare. I did not see Clayton much at all because he was spending most of his time talking to Mr. Otis, and when I did see him at meals he just looked at me.

It was late at night on the eighth of May, and I was in Aunt Eusie's room playing our next-to-the-last hand of cards for the night, when we hit the snag. "I think I just won four hundred and fifty dollars," she said right away. We only had three more cards to play in that hand, so we did that and then we collected the cards together and went outside. There was a lot of moving around going on, men coming up the stairs from the bottom deck and running back and forth along the balcony and getting their goods out of their rooms and then going on up to the top balcony. The crew went around turning off lanterns to prevent a fire, so it got to be more or less dark, and all the while the steam whistle kept blowing. We watched by the balcony for a while, and then Aunt Eusie said I should go and get what I had in my room, which was two shirts, a coat, under-drawers, a voyager's hat, a knife, waterproof boots, and my volume of Shakespeare, all in one bag, and then come back to her room and finish the game, which was fine with me. Before I could leave, Clayton came along carrying everything from the two of us and looking as mad as a pirate. The fact of sinking had put him a little on the edge, no matter he was a good swimmer.

"I want to see you, Henry," he said, and Aunt Eusie

told us we could go in her room. When we got inside, Clayton shut the door and told me to sit down, which I did. "I'm wrought, Henry," he said. "You want to know what I'm wrought about? I'm wrought about the state of your soul, that's what I'm wrought about. It goes hard for hypocrites before the Lord, you know it does, Henry." He kept looking deep in my eyes, which made me think about the Reverend Mr. Sweetvarnish looking for the demon in his cow. "False witness is another thing can bring you to the judgment, you know that too, don't you, Henry."

"Yes, I do," I said.

"Hypocrites and liars are an abomination to the Lord, and it is his pleasure to spew them out of his mouth."

I shook my head yes, though I was not completely sure as to his second part.

"Well, how are you going to make it right?"

"Clayton, I'm not sure what you are talking about," I said.

He took my poems out of his pocket and put them right back in again. "You know what. These."

"I didn't think you had copies," I said.

"Well, there are some things you just don't know, and isn't that just a proper shame. Clemmy wrote them out for me in her own hand, and I just showed them to the Reverend Mr. Otis not five minutes ago, and he started to laugh, so naturally I looked at them to find out why, which is as plain as the nose on your face, namely that they are nothing more or less than mockeries of sacred things."

"Clemmy and I have a friendly feud is all," I said. "If I had thought she was going to believe those poems, I would never have written them."

"You have a contentious spirit in you, Henry," Clayton said, "and that's the truth."

"I can't dispute that with you, Clayton," I said. "I know I presume too much on mercy."

"Don't joke, Henry. You made a genuine profane mockery out of the sacred name of love."

"I didn't intend her to believe me," I said. "She just didn't take care to read them. She saw the word love, so she thought they were true love poems."

"Not to say you wrote them out in red ink."

"No, we don't have any red ink. It was brown."

About this time the snag we were hung up on broke, no doubt from the weight of the boat and all the water in it, and the current started to move us back down the river.

"Is that your word that you have to say to me at a time like this?" he said, nodding his head up and down. "You used brown ink, which you know very well looks red in the dark, and that makes everything right? Is that how you plead before the throne of the Lord?"

"This is just a boat, Clayton."

He stopped nodding his head and began shaking it. "Oh, how wrong you are, Henry. We cannot now forget what this boat is, what's happening to this boat. You and I both may soon enough stand before the throne of the Lord to answer to his judgment. And I will tell you this, no matter what happens she will never find out how you lied to her from my lips, that I swear. I could send you home, Henry. You know which one of us is in charge of which one of us. There's boats going down this river every day. You see them."

Just then the boiler blew up, the door jumped off its hinges and fell in the room, and we didn't talk any more for a little while.

⟦ *Chapter IV* ⟧

THE BOILER BLOWING UP turned everybody earnest. There were ladders on both sides of the boat going from the top balcony to the roof, and people climbed up them as quick as they could, the crew scrambling along with everybody else. Aunt Eusie and Mr. Otis and Clayton and I were about the last ones up because Mr. Otis had thirty-six books of different sizes that needed to be packed just right to fit in his case. Mostly everybody crowded toward the back end of the boat, as far as they could get away from the hole, so we went to the front end and camped right behind the pilothouse.

There was no steam to blow the whistle any more, so it was pretty peaceful and quiet up there except for the noise of the horses clumping back and forth on the main deck. They had been let out of the stables so they could swim to shore if they had to.

This was the first sinking I was ever a party to, except for the one at the beginning of *The Tempest*. In that play the sailors get down on their hands and knees and start praying, and the passengers run around waiting to drown in the next odd minute, and the ship stands half on its end, and everything goes to wrack straightaway.

With the *Jane Sure* it was altogether different and

slower. The boat just got lower and lower in the water, all the while turning slowly around in circles and sliding along with the current, so if you lay down on your back you could see the stars making a wheel over you. I did not see much reason to worry, the bottom of the boat being more or less flat and the river no more than fifteen or twenty feet deep where we were. The only way to sink to the roof there would have been to find a hole in the river and anchor over it.

Aunt Eusie and I played some more hands of cards by the moonlight, but her heart was not in it, or mine either, so after a while we stopped. I was thinking about her chest of goods down in the storage room on the left-hand side of the boat, which was the way the boat was tipping, and I could see that she was thinking about it, too.

Mr. Otis and Clayton were talking about Paris, France. Clayton was of the opinion that, excepting for the land of China, the place that needed true religion the most in the world was that city. One big trouble standing in the way, he said, was that everybody in France spoke a foreign language. "If everybody there talked English, then everybody would understand the same words and we could all read the same Bible," he said, which of course is true enough. "Still, now that I have received the call, I am ready to study any foreign tongue at all, if I am led that way." Mr. Otis had been in Paris once, when he was a boy, and he told about it. From what he said, it sounded like a city that was various to a degree. Clayton said it sounded to him like a wheat field ripe for the harvest, and Mr. Otis said that it was, and also that it was a vineyard ready for the pressing.

I asked Aunt Eusie about Buffalo, and she told me stories about the city and about the people who lived on the same street as her stepfather. You would have thought, just listening to her and looking at her, that the roof of the *Jane Sure* was her front sitting room, or maybe a private park, she acted so much at home there. Even Clayton left off his conversation and listened to her.

We stopped talking when the boat laid into the right-hand bank of the river. There was an oak tree sticking out from the bluff right there, and the boat got squeezed like a wedge between it and the bottom, back end first. Right after we hit, the captain came out the back door of the pilothouse wearing his Sunday captain's suit. "What happened?" he said, which was a question there was no need to answer.

We all stood up, Aunt Eusie too. "You may keep the four hundred and fifty dollars you owe me until we get to Saint Joseph, if you don't mind, Captain," she said. "In fact, I wish you would."

He looked up at the sky and started to walk away toward the back of the boat. "The *Jane Sure* is having her share of troubles," he said, "but at least she hasn't sunk." Before he got to the word "sunk," he was already ten feet away and walking fast. The boat had pretty much of a tilt to it, but he walked in a very dignified manner, as if he thought it was as level as a prairie.

"He's going to try to get your ten dollars and not pay the four hundred and fifty," I said to Aunt Eusie.

48

She looked at me and made her eyes big. "Well, well, Henry, your dear old Aunt Eusie is certainly surprised to hear that," she said, but you could tell from her voice that she was not surprised at all.

"He has to pay you in the end, doesn't he?" I asked her.

"No," she said, "but he will. He's an honorable man."

"Could you take him to court if he didn't?"

She shook her head. "I wouldn't anyway, not for two times four hundred and fifty. But don't worry about it."

"What can he say if he doesn't allow that the boat sank?"

Aunt Eusie smiled. "He can say that on the night of May 8 the *Jane Sure* got so low in the water that she could no longer move, but that she certainly did not sink."

I made up my mind right then to go down into the storage room where Aunt Eusie's chest was and rescue it before Captain Fountain got it out from under water and gave it to her as if it was his to give. There were some lanterns I could see coming along the shore from Saint Joseph, and they made me hurry, even though I was sure that no one would come on board until light.

The boat was leaning to the left quite a bit, so I went down on the right-hand side, where the ladders were laying in against the boat, instead of the left-hand side, where they were hanging out over the water. Once I got to the top balcony I felt along the wall to the stairs and went down to the middle balcony. I was entirely out of the moonlight then, and also in under ceilings, so it was as dark as a cave. I felt around and unhooked a lantern, expecting I might find a match or some other way to light it when I got to the steam engine room. I was sure that a lot of the bottom deck was under water, and maybe all of it, so I took off my shoes and hung them around my neck, and then I went down.

I had made up my mind that if the water in the left-hand storeroom was up as high as my neck, I would not hunt for Aunt Eusie's chest. The deck was dry under the stairs, and I stood there thinking about what the best way would be to get into the storeroom. Just then Mr. Nowac came around from the front of the boat with a stable lantern in his hand that was lit. I have to confess that when I saw him I thought he was probably down there to steal something. I believe that he knew what I was thinking, too. More than likely he could see it on my face. Most white men would have thought the same thing, but it still shames me to remember it, because he was a true man and ready to prove it. He was there to get three bolts of silk he was bringing north to sell and trade.

I never asked him, naturally, but I believe that when he first saw me he thought I was a thief, too, poking around and trying to steal whatever was loose. I some-times wonder if there wasn't a real thief down there somewhere watching both of us and laughing. For a minute he just looked at me, which made me feel peculiar. "I'm looking for a match to light this lantern with," I said. He didn't answer me anything, except maybe nodding his head a little bit. I told him that a friend of mine, Miss Eusebia Otis of Buffalo, New York, had a trunk in the storeroom on the other side of the boat and I wanted to get it out.

"That side is deep under water," he said in his high, soft voice, and I told him that I knew that, but I thought I'd try anyway, and asked him if he'd light my lantern from his, which he did. After that I offered to help him get his goods, which turned out to be in the near storage room, with only about a foot of water in it, and he said no, he'd rather go in there by himself.

From where we were it was only a few steps to the engine room, and we went there. High up in the front wall, across from the furnace, there were two small trap doors, one into each storeroom, with ladders leading up to them. Right away Mr. Nowac went and climbed up the right-hand ladder. He was a big man, and he made the ladder creak like he was going to pull the whole wall down.

The engine room did not really look so bad, considering that the boiler had blown up. The wood bin was split open, and there were sticks everywhere and broken glass and pieces of machinery hanging different places, and the walls were blotched over red from the rusty water that blew out of the boiler. Also, there was a horse standing by the bin, probably making believe to himself that it was a stable. All the other horses were clumping around outside, at the back right corner of the boat, which was the highest place. Still, considering the noise and the shake the boat took when the boiler blew up, the room looked more or less neat. Naturally a lot of the mess was covered up with water which was real cold, but not so cold you couldn't get used to it. Being barefoot, I worried a little bit about what I might step on.

The trap doors had hook latches, and Mr. Nowac just opened his up and crawled through. I climbed up behind him with my lantern. There was a platform inside, and a narrow stair leading down into the storeroom. Mr. Nowac was already down inside when I poked my head through, and I put my lantern on the platform as a high light. The storeroom floor was somewhat lower than the engine-room floor, and had about two feet of water on it, but his bolts of silk were up on a dry shelf, wrapped in cloth, with a yellow label wired to them. He picked all three of them up and carried them over to the stairs, splashing through the water as he came.

He was a striking man, not just for his size but for his face, especially his smoky-looking eyes. Just the difference of him from everybody else I knew was enough to make me watch him and think about him. When he came back through the water with his arms around the three bolts of silk I thought back to Hanna, and I saw him in my mind carrying her away in the middle of the night with both arms around her. I could feature him holding her against him to smother her, or holding her up and kissing her like a father, or shaking her hard in the air with both his hands and throwing her off a cliff. All three of those fancies passed through my mind as fast as it took for him to make ten steps.

I got off the platform and went down to the bottom of the ladder so if he wanted to hand me down the bolts, which were heavy, he could, but he didn't. When he reached the floor he propped them up against a rung and opened them one by one to make sure they were all right. One was gold-colored, one was almost black with something sewed in it, and one was white with different-colored flowers. They were all three pearls of great price to him, as any fool could see.

We got into the second storeroom the same way as the first, and just as easy. There were not many items in it that I could see, but there was a lot of water. It looked to be up to my shoulders on the deep side. "I don't know how big the chest is, or what it looks like," I said, "but it's sure to have a tag with her name on it."

"Do you know it is down there?" he said.

"I was with her when she told the captain where it was," I said. "It's maybe too heavy to float."

I put the lantern on the platform for a high light, and since I did not want to get my clothes wet, I shucked them off before I went down. Once I got my whole self in the water and started moving around, it was more or less tolerable. The trick was not to pay a lot of mind to the way the water felt, but to hunt after the chest. I expected that it would be under water, and maybe even pressed under something else that was under water.

I went along the more shallow side of the room, looking at the high shelves and feeling around the low ones with my feet. I had a clear notion, for no good reason, of what the chest would look like. I was sure that it would be made out of dark wood, and have leather handles and corners. It turned out in the end that I was wrong.

When I was done with the shallow side, I went over

to the deep side and found the chest right away, wedged in the corner behind a canvas bag full of picks and shovels. I had to slide the chest sideways before I could pull it out. This work required me to have my arms under water, and sometimes my head, but I did not think about it or even feel it very much.

The chest did not float up when I got it loose, but I could move it around under water. For a minute I just stood still and tried to figure out how I was going to get it up the stairs to the platform, and then down the ladder on the other side and into the engine room. There was no way I could do it by myself, and I did not want to ask Mr. Nowac to come down and help me. Then I saw all at once what to do. There was a loading door at the far end of the room, and this door was inside-bolted. All I had to do was haul the chest over to it, open the door up, and pull the chest around to the high side of the boat, which is what I did. Naturally, I did not put on my clothes to do this.

When I got it to the place I wanted it, I tipped it up against the rail so the water would run out. It was a very big chest, with double-fist bronze handles, copper corners, and a lid that came halfway down over the side. All the seams were tight around the lid, so even when it was all the way under water it could only get half full, and the top drawers stayed dry. I stood next to it for a minute, more or less, just enjoying the pleasure of watching the water run out of it.

I was about to go back the way I had come and get my clothes on, when Clayton leaned out over the first balcony rail and asked me what I was doing standing out in the open looking like I did. "Don't answer me. Don't do anything but go get your clothes on," he said right away. "I'm not going to talk to you again until you come back up on the roof with all your clothes on."

"I didn't want to get them wet, and I'm no colder this way," I said. "The water's up to your shoulders in there. You couldn't even keep a hat dry, I don't think."

"Is that Miss Otis's chest? Don't tell me. You're a lunatic, Henry, just a lunatic, and there's nothing else to it, and we might just as well get used to it right now."

"It was the best way I could see to get it," I said. "There was no profit in getting the half of my clothes wet when there was no need."

"You disgrace your whole family for a stranger," Clayton said. "Get in under something. I don't want to talk to you."

"Nobody can see me," I said, which was clearly true because the moon was already down on the other side of the boat, and it was only just beginning to get light. Clayton wasn't a dozen feet away, and even he could hardly see me. To give him his fair due, however, he had some reason to be nervous, because there was a crowd of people gathered on the shore, and they could have seen me if the moon had been up and shining on that side. I was curious to know how many of those people were Presbyterians, who would surely rejoice to see their new preacher step in among them, for as the saying is, "The tread of the prophets lifteth up the hearts of the righteous," but I did not bring this up to Clayton, who had his mind fixed upon the danger of people seeing me as I was. And, surely, the crowd was getting bigger and bigger all the time. People were coming by wagonloads to see the wreck, and I would have been a fair-sized fool if I had not said goodbye to Clayton right then, and gone back around through the storeroom, which I did so that I could lock the door again, and climbed up to where my clothes were and put them on. The lantern was still up there, burning, but Mr. Nowac was gone. In five minutes' time I was pretty well steamed off dry, so I did not get my clothes wet when I put them on again. Then I sat by the lantern thinking about the chest draining away, and about Aunt Eusie. I also pretended I had a cup of coffee I was drinking and a cigar I was smoking. If Clayton had seen me there he would have had me certified a lunatic, no mistake, and taken off to the asylum for a long stay.

When I went back out on the deck it was getting light. I could make out the wagons up on top of the bluff, which was about twenty feet or maybe a little bit less over the water, but I could still hear things better than I could see them because of the morning mist. People were calling back and forth between the bluff and the roof, and somewhere among the wagons there was a little girl being chased around and laughing. It sounded like she was nearly out of breath, but having a fine time and nobody stopping her. And it was plain that whoever was chasing her was not catching her.

Aunt Eusie's chest was pretty much drained out now, and I made up my mind to get it onto the high balcony. I was sure that when it got full daylight they would stretch a gangway between that balcony and the bluff, because they were more or less the same height now, which as it turned out is what they did. There were two brass rails like tracks on the bottom side of the chest, and the stairs were not too steep, so I could slide it up in stages by pushing from the bottom and resting every little bit.

I left the chest at the top of the stairs with the label showing and went up to the roof to look for Aunt Eusie and tell her what I had done. You could see everything now, even if the sun was not yet up. Everybody on the roof was busy and moving around, and some of the men were getting off the boat by climbing into the tree we were wedged under and going through it to the bluff. A baker had come out from Saint Joseph with a wagon-load of bread, and he was selling it. I saw one man with two loaves of bread under his arm coming back through the tree and onto the boat again and passing it around among his friends. The kitchen on the *Jane Sure* was pretty much under water.

Aunt Eusie was standing near the pilothouse looking across at the bluff, and when she saw me she came over to me and took a hold of my hand and held it for a little bit. "Clayton told me you got my chest and I appreciate it, Henry," she said. Clayton was with her, and he said he was glad to see me dressed again and hoped I had not gotten a chill. He tried to sound like our father, which was kind of him.

With the light, some of the men on the roof started to climb down to see after their goods. Those who had horses, naturally, were among the first ones down. Mr. Couteaux, the French trader, had two horses, and he went down and took Mr. Nowac with him. They walked right by me going to the ladder, but Mr. Nowac paid me no mind at all. I told Aunt Eusie about going into the storerooms with him, and about the bolts of silk he had.

"He must have a family of women," she said.

"If he's got silk goods, it's for trade," Clayton said, which turned out to be the case. Mr. Otis thought he was probably carrying one bolt for each one of his wives. "That could really be true if he's a chief," Clayton said. "Three wives is few for an Indian chief."

All the while Aunt Eusie, who had let loose of my hand, kept looking across at the bluff, and I thought probably she was looking to see Mr. Johnson, so I asked her if she expected him to be in Saint Joseph.

"I wrote him on April 20, right after we bought our tickets," she said. "He does business in Kanesville, chiefly, which is five or six days from here, and he may not even have received my letter yet."

"Maybe it's in the mail sack in the captain's office," I said.

She just nodded her head and smiled and began to talk about another matter. "My wedding dress is in the lid of the chest, Henry, wrapped in cheesecloth and gentian paper. I want to go into Saint Joseph now, if I can, and find my uncle, Mr. Pewbrace. Since it's been in the water, the sooner we get the chest open, the better. In the bottom of it are two small nets of tinted camphor. I don't have any notion of what water does to bags of camphor, or if the tint will come out, but if it does it is likely to harm my goods, and some of them are very old and fine. It's going to be a sunny day. Here is the key to the chest. As soon as they put a gangway

58

up, you and Clayton carry the chest off the boat, get the lid open, and spread everything in it out to dry. That piece of prairie over there looks like a good place to do that. If you can't get the lock to work, just go ahead and pry the lid up any way you can. Mr. Otis and I will certainly be back before the end of the day and fetch you. Of course I'll pay you both for your kindness."

"We'll do it out of the goodness of our hearts," Clayton said. "Besides, you'll need to keep all the money you have if the captain won't pay his debts."

"Honorable men always pay what they owe, if they can," she said. "And don't worry about us finding you. If that piece of prairie turns out to be no good for the purpose, just find some other sunny place. We'll find you. And maybe you can do something about drying out the chest, too. And buy some bread from that wagon over there, so you don't go hungry. I've been smelling it for an hour."

Right away, Aunt Eusie and the Reverend Mr. Otis went to the back end of the boat and walked through the tree and over to the bluff. It was a strange sight to me, because I had never seen a woman in a tree before. After we saw that they were safe on the bluff we got our hand pack and went down to the chest. In about an hour, or maybe less than that, they put out the gangway between the boat and the bluff and Clayton and I half ran and half walked, with the chest between us, to the piece of prairie where Aunt Eusie expected us to go. The key fit the lock and turned, but I had to go back to the boat and get a bar to pry up the lid, which was leather on the outside and carpet on the inside, with a layer of copper in between, because the bottom was swollen tight against it.

The chest smelled like a mortician parlor, only stronger, and put me in mind of cholera funerals. The camphor was whole, but the dye had come out and colored some goods, mostly on the bottom. The main item to save was Aunt Eusie's wedding dress, which I took out of the lid right after I got rid of the camphor. The gentian paper around it was wet, but it peeled away in one piece. The cheesecloth had splotches of purple on it in places, but the wedding dress was pure white except for the apron part, which had some flecks on it here and there. I spread everything out on the grass, including the cheesecloth. After that I went and threw the gentian paper in the river, and at the same time I washed the color off my hands.

In the same drawer with the wedding dress there was a book of drawings that Mr. Johnson had made for Aunt Eusie and sent to her. There were drawings of flowers and trees from around the Council Bluffs, and a picture of the Bluffs from across the Missouri River. There were also some pictures of Indians, trappers, and neighbors from Kanesville. The pictures were very clear and fine, and at the bottom of each one it said what it was.

We took the trunk apart as much as we could, and then Clayton went and got a tin can of soup and some bread. They tasted as good as anything I ever ate. Clayton was very good-natured about all of this work, which was a true virtue for him because it went against his feelings to spread anybody's goods in the sun, especially a lady's.

The smell of camphor went rising up off those goods like a fragrant sacrifice unto the nostrils of the Lord, as the Reverend Mr. Sweetvarnish says about the Sunday offering, and we waited for Aunt Eusie to find us. We weren't two hundred yards from where the boat was sunk in the mud, and we were on the side of a slope, so there was no way she could miss us. She and Mr. Otis came back a little bit after noon. There was no word about Mr. Johnson in Saint Joseph, and Aunt Eusie didn't pay too much mind to the apron of her wedding dress having purple flecks on it.

〖 Chapter V 〗

AUNT EUSIE AND MR. OTIS had her uncle, Mr. Titus Pewbrace, with them to fetch the chest and us into town. Mr. Pewbrace had a high, black Brittany Carriage and fine-looking horses. He was a tall man with a lumpy forehead and bushy eyebrows, so when he looked at you it was like being watched out of a tree. He always wore black French-cut suits every day no matter where he was, and at night he put on Chinese pajamas, yellow or orange, and a long silk robe with a decorated belt and a stuffed collar. Day or night it was hard to keep your eyes off of him.

He told us right away about what he was born to do. "My life work," he said, "is to spread joy and put aside ignorance among all my neighbors." He was also very kind to his livestock. He fed his horses and mules grains and grass both, summer and winter. He was a tall man, and except for his eyebrows he didn't have a hair on his head. "I can hatch bird eggs in my eyebrows, and in fact I often do," he said. "The trouble is, once the birds hatch out they keep falling in my lap."

He and Clayton and I got acquainted while we were folding goods to load in the carriage, and before we were started to town Clayton had already told him about his plans to be a preacher. "When the boiler blew up, right in that sound I could hear the voice of the Lord," he said. Mr. Pewbrace was very happy about that. "Clayton, my friend, you will no doubt help me to become a finer man," he said, and he spent most of the way into Saint Joseph finding out everything he could about Clayton's plans for the future. Clayton told him also about wanting to marry Clemmy Burke, and what a fine girl she was.

"I haven't asked her yet, but I have faith she will say yes to my plea," he said, which seemed likely at the time and gave Clayton, as I believe, many hours of happy visions.

Saint Joseph is only 160 acres big, and the bulk of the people there in the spring are on their way to somewhere else, most of them to California and some to Iowa and the Dakotas. The streets are full of traders and Indians and people still wearing their eastern suits, and you hear a lot of talk in French. The town was laid out by a Frenchman, Mr. Joseph Robidoux, five years ago. Before he came, it was called Blacksnake Hills, and it was nothing but a trading post. It is a good location to plant a town. The bluff moves back from the river at that place, and there is a fine level plat that drains into the river, but still not so low as to get flooded every spring. There are already some brick houses there, and a fine large brick courthouse. The Saint Andrews parsonage, where we stayed, is a fine and substantial place made of wood. Mr. Robidoux's aim, they say, is to have a white prince from France visit the town before he dies. I got to see him the next day after we got there.

63

He was walking along the street, leading a string of horses he had to sell. He looked to be somewhere between sixty and seventy, and very robust.

So it turned out that, after all, we got to Saint Joseph the day the boat was supposed to get there, which was Tuesday, May 9, eight days from Saint Louis. Aunt Eusie wanted to make a dash for Kanesville starting Thursday morning. There was a stage on Saturday, but there was no reason to wait for it because Mr. Pewbrace had an overland wagon all ready. It was a light wagon with wide iron wheels for the mud, and you could sleep under cover in it if you had to. He was happy to take Clayton and me along if one of us would ride a horse, and he even offered to loan us one of his own, but Clayton decided to buy a horse instead, and along with it a weather hat and a shot bag too, which he could get the next day.

Between Saint Joseph and the Council Bluffs are one hundred and fifty miles. The stage makes the trip in four days when the weather is good, and Mr. Pewbrace said he knew the country and could do it in the same. So everybody was pretty lively all Tuesday afternoon drinking coffee and eating cakes left by the ladies of the Andrews church as a welcome to Mr. Otis and looking all over the house and making out plans for Wednesday. Late in the afternoon it turned cold, so we lit the fires that were laid out downstairs and had tea with rum in it that Mr. Pewbrace made. The parsonage had nine fireplaces. Everybody felt at home.

It happens sometimes that you meet a man and right

64

away you know you can trust him. That's how I felt about Mr. Pewbrace, so I told him about the four hundred and fifty dollars that Captain Fountain owed Aunt Eusie. It turned out he knew Captain Fountain from Baltimore. They had sailed on the same ship together. "All of a sudden I feel the need to go this evening and renew my acquaintance with Thomas Hanford Fountain," he said. "It will be a cause for rejoicing in my soul, and no doubt in his soul, too, when we look each other in the eyes once again and speak a manly word or two. Speaking in a deep and sober voice, I will confess to him the grim truth that we were never close friends. After that beginning, we shall give ourselves up to mirth for a while, laughing at one another's little jokes, and then I shall tell him about the joy every good man feels when he pays his debts, and he will agree that I am right, and hand over the cash. How does that sound to you? Is it a good plan? Does it make sense?"

"It sounds fine to me," I said.

"Then we shall follow it, unless some other plan comes to mind," he said, "and you will come with me to lend moral weight to the occasion. I have always needed help in that regard."

He asked Clayton at dinner if he wanted to go with us, but Clayton said no. There was a prayer meeting and social hour at the Andrews church to welcome Mr. Otis, and he wanted to be there to help with the singing. "Besides that," he said, "I want to ask among the congregation and see how to send my brother back to

Saint Louis the fastest way, in case I decide that he ought to go." He likely thought he was doing me a kindness, making me a better and stronger person, by reminding me that he had rights over me, but he did not need to do it. I had not forgotten that he could send me back home if he wanted to, or make me stay behind on our cousin John's farm when we got to Kanesville, or even leave me in Saint Joseph with Mr. Otis.

Mr. Pewbrace and I left the parsonage at the same time everybody else did, right after dinner, and started walking to the Hotel Mansion House. "I know Captain Fountain doesn't own a house in Saint Joseph, and he can't be sleeping on his boat tonight, so he must be there," Mr. Pewbrace said. Mr. Pewbrace lived there, too. He had the whole top floor, six rooms, all to himself. "That many rooms must cost a lot of money a week," I said, and he said yes, that they did, but that there was no need for him to worry about it because he had plenty. "The plain truth is that I'm rolling in the stuff," he said. "Wealth grows on me like mold in a damp room." He did not sound proud of his money, as people sometimes do, but at the same time he seemed to take more pleasure in it than most people do. I remember getting a dollar for my birthday when I was seven, and feeling the same way about that one dollar as he did about all of his.

I asked him how he became rich, and he told me. For fifteen years he had owned partner's shares in three different ships that sailed out of Baltimore. Before that, he had been first mate on a whaler out of New Bedford, in Massachusetts. He never was a captain except for one day, when the captain over him drowned. "Right after I finished reading the funeral service, I gave his coat and rank to the cook, who was exactly his size."

"Why didn't you want to be captain yourself?" I asked him.

"I did," he said, "but the cook had been a captain once before and lost his rank in disgrace, so he needed it more than I did. He was a good captain, too. We were out another ten months."

When we got to the hotel Mr. Pewbrace found out what room Captain Fountain was in and we went up the stairs to it. The captain was in, but he was not very glad to see us.

"Miss Otis and I had a clear agreement," he said before he even got the door shut. "I told her in the best way I knew how that the *Jane Sure* would never sink, but she had to have it her way and bet money on it at usurious odds."

Mr. Pewbrace sat down on a bench at the foot of Captain Fountain's bed and nodded his head. "It is a fine thing when two people can reach a watertight understanding," he said. "Deep places speak to deep places, twin souls drink from the same cup, two springs flow together into a single river, and so forth. Miss Otis, I know, remembers your conversation with great pleasure."

Captain Fountain nodded his head and smiled. He had beautiful front teeth. "As long as she doesn't misunderstand me, I'm ready to forget the wager altogether. I don't like to wager with women anyway. I only did it because she insisted."

"Hanford, you are just as fine a man today as you were on the day we first met. If I had taken the time to know you better then, I would no doubt have become a wiser man by now."

Captain Fountain offered us some mineral water from a bottle on the bedside table, but Mr. Pewbrace said he never drank after dinner, and I also declined. "I come for another kind of refreshment entirely," Mr. Pewbrace said.

"What's that?" the captain asked.

"The cool water of justice," Mr. Pewbrace said. "What shall I tell you about our purpose in coming to visit you? Shall I tell you that Henry and I are here to celebrate the good luck which is being enjoyed tonight by the top half of your boat?"

"The entire passenger-cabin part of my boat is high and dry," Mr. Fountain said. "And that's more than half."

"Measured how, by weight or bulk?" Mr. Pewbrace asked, but Captain Fountain didn't have time to answer, because Mr. Pewbrace asked him another question right away. "But we don't want to do arithmetic, do we? Especially fractions. That's for children, don't you think? Is the boat insured?"

"That is a private matter between myself and my partners," Captain Fountain said.

"Hanford," Mr. Pewbrace said, "you have no idea how glad I am to hear that you do not have to stand alone in your hour of trouble. Partners are a rich blessing."

68

Captain Fountain took out a cigar and pointed it at me. "This boy here."

"You mean Henry?"

"That boy right there, I mean."

"Henry."

"Him. He heard the wager as clear as I did. I warned your aunt, didn't I, Henry?"

"She's not my aunt," I said.

"Well, whatever she is," the captain said, and bit off the end of his cigar and spit the piece in the fireplace. Mr. Pewbrace took out his pipe and opened up a knife and began peeling out the bowl and putting the peelings in his pocket.

"My friend Henry is only telling the truth as an honest boy should, Hanford. Miss Otis is not his aunt, she is my niece, the only child of my sister, and one of the prettiest babies I ever saw, and she has come here to be married after faithfully nursing her stepfather for twenty years. Not to boast, I arranged the wedding. She is going to marry my former business partner. You see, after I came here I went into trading. You are smiling, I think."

"I'm not smiling," the captain said. It was true, he was not smiling, but you could see his teeth.

"Oh," Mr. Pewbrace said, standing up, "I was hoping that we might have a little innocent laughter together, but never mind."

Captain Fountain was watching him peel out his pipe like it was some kind of magic act. "I have to meet somebody in a little while from now," he said.

Mr. Pewbrace paid this no mind at all. In fact, he sat

69

down again. It looked like he was planning on staying in that room forever. "People think I'm rich, Hanford. They point their fingers at me on the street. Mothers tell their little children to look and see the man with all the money. The common herd, as you know, is often wrong, but in this case it is dead right. Would you prefer it if I didn't talk about money?"

"You can talk about whatever you want to talk about, except that I have somebody waiting for me downstairs."

"When you have a great deal of money, you sometimes miss the poor but simple sea life. The soul of a sailor is sometimes made heavy by the vain pomp of the world, I often say."

Captain Fountain's cigar was already lit, but he lit it again.

"As a rule," Mr. Pewbrace said, "people only talk about money when they don't have it. When you are a hissing and a byword for wealth, you usually keep pretty quiet about it."

"I have to go," the captain said.

Mr. Pewbrace looked over at me. "Tell him about the stains, Henry."

"Some of the things in Aunt Eusie's trunk have gotten stained," I said, "and her wedding-dress apron has purple spots all over it."

Mr. Pewbrace nodded his head. "My friend Henry is right, Hanford. Many of the purple splotches he speaks of are small, of course, but they do catch the eye. Did I tell you I was here to make an offer?"

"The worst you can say is that the boat ran aground,"

the captain said. "I'll never say it sank because that would be a lie. Go down along the river and look at it."

"Why pay out money when you don't have to?" Mr. Pewbrace said. "Here is my offer. I propose to pay my niece the money you owe her out of my own large reserves. That way she will get what is coming to her, and you will not have to put out a penny."

"You can do whatever you want," Captain Fountain said.

Mr. Pewbrace stood up. "Excellent," he said. "Then our business is at an end."

"What will you tell her when you give it to her?"

"I have it all planned out, Hanford. First I will hand her the envelope, and then I will say, speaking slowly in a voice which is known and loved by many, 'My dear Eusebia, inside this envelope you will find the four hundred and fifty dollars which you are owed. Go right away today and buy yourself another chest full of linens without splotches.' She will then ask me where the money comes from, and I will tell her."

"Then she will give it right back to you," Captain Fountain said.

Mr. Pewbrace shook his head. "Eusebia Louise Otis is a woman without a spot of foolish pride, Hanford. No, she will take the money, kiss me on the cheek, and go out to the store and buy her goodies."

"But at least it will be a private matter between the two of you," Captain Fountain said. "With, naturally, Henry here knowing about it, too."

"Not a chance, Hanford. She will tell everyone she can. She may even write a poem in my honor and set it to music, using the tune of some popular hymn, and sing it on the streets. Everyone in Saint Joseph will know why she thinks I am such a fine fellow."

"And what will people say about me?" Captain Fountain said. His cigar had gone out by now, but he didn't light it up again.

"That depends on who is talking," Mr. Pewbrace said. "Some people will say that you are lucky, and others will say that you have four hundred and fifty dollars that rightfully belong to a sweet and innocent woman. Everybody, on the other hand, will agree that I am a saint, or something similar, and of course they will be right."

The captain sat down, and then he changed his mind and stood up again. "All that happened on the river last night, when you come down to it, is that the *Jane Sure* got lower in the water. Still, I would be grateful if you would put off giving Miss Otis the money until tomorrow. Let me talk about the matter to my partners."

"I never do anything in haste," Mr. Pewbrace said, smiling in a very kindly way. They shook hands, then, and we left and started walking back to the parsonage. It was already dark. Mr. Pewbrace had a more or less sad face as we went along, so I did not ask him anything and we did not talk. When we got back to the parsonage nobody was home yet. The Andrews church was right across the street and it was all lit up, even to there being a lantern lit at the door and another in the steeple, and nobody was coming out, so we knew it would be a wait.

I told Mr. Pewbrace that it was kind of him to wait

with me, but that I did not need company, and that he should feel free to go back to the hotel. He just kept sitting. "Mr. Johnson will make Miss Otis a good husband," he said after a while. "He and I were in trade together for ten years, from the time I came out here from Baltimore. He's a few years younger than she is, perhaps three or four, but that doesn't make any difference. He's a good man."

"She looks to be all ready to marry him," I said.

"She trusts me," he said. "Captain Fountain does not. I think I did not help him tonight to become a higher and more noble creature. That fact turns me thoughtful."

"I bet he pays Aunt Eusie the money he owed her, and that's a good thing," I said.

He shook his head. "I could see my day's work better if I was in my pajamas. My mind would then fill up with ideas, and I would see clearly what I had to do to help the captain to walk bravely forward, thereby gaining a clearer and a more beautiful view of things. Life is short, Henry, and we have to do as much good as we can in it."

"I don't think you should worry about doing good," I said. "It looks to me like you do a lot of good."

"Well, I don't, but I am cheered to find out that you think I do, because I am planning to have a funeral some day at which women faint, strong men sob in one another's arms, dogs howl, and everyone talks about what a wonderful human being I was." He looked at me. "Does your brother Clayton seriously want to send you back to Saint Louis? Should I talk to him?"

"That would be very kind of you," I said. "I don't think he wants to do it, but I don't know for sure. He gets ideas."

"It will be simple. I will look down at him with my arrow-blue eyes, and he will look up at me with his baby-blue eyes, and suddenly he will see clearly that I am standing on top of a high tower of money, and that therefore I must be full of wisdom."

He got up right away, and walked across the street and went into the church. I don't know what he said to Clayton, or what corner he got him into, but when the party was over at the church and they all came back to the house together Clayton told me that he was going to forgive me for being bad on the boat and let me come on with him to Kanesville. Aunt Eusie was glad to hear this, she said, because she wanted us both to be at the wedding.

⟦ *Chapter VI* ⟧

T HE NEXT MORNING, as a sign that he was forgiving me for my sins, Clayton gave me his rifle and a lecture on how to look after it. He had made up his mind, he said, to buy a new one in Saint Joseph that would shoot long-range. The gun was clean, and he had stayed up late into the night setting the trigger fine for me, so that all I would have to do was touch it and the gun would go off, providing it was loaded.

While he was giving me warnings of one kind and another, and showing me this part and that on the gun, he kept looking out of the window, so I knew the spirit of leaving had a hold on him. In fact, it had a hold on us all, Aunt Eusie because of Mr. Johnson waiting for her in Kanesville, as she supposed, and Clayton because of rescuing Hanna, and me for both reasons. Mr. Pewbrace, the fourth member of our party, was a first-class mover no matter what, and for him it was always the sooner the better. Not to put too fine a point on it, all of us were already on the road to Kanesville in our hearts, except of course for the Reverend Mr. Otis.

Mr. Pewbrace came over from the Hotel Mansion House around six-thirty with his kit all packed and in his wagon. With him he brought a side of bacon and twenty eggs and a list for Mr. Otis of the ten best houses in town to be invited to dinner at. Behind him not two minutes later came a messenger with the money from Captain Fountain, four hundred and forty dollars in ten-dollar gold pieces in a leather bag with a receipt tied to it with "ALL CLAIMS PAID IN FULL" written on it. Aunt Eusie signed her name and asked the messenger to sit down to breakfast, which he did.

Now that she had the money, Aunt Eusie was more or less required to buy some goods to fill up her chest. "I'll spend half of it," she said, "and Mr. Johnson and I together will decide what to do with the rest." It was certainly a petty thing, Captain Fountain holding back the ten dollars, as if he had won the bet, too, but Aunt Eusie did not bring it up and nobody else did, either. In fact, she had charity for him. "It must be terrible to lose a boat," she said. "Even if it isn't your fault, and you have partners to share the loss, as I expect Captain Fountain does, it's hard on a man's spirit."

"He only lost the bottom half," Mr. Pewbrace said.

"That's an unkind remark, Uncle Titus," she said.

Clayton left right after breakfast to buy his rifle, horse, hat, and shot. Aunt Eusie stayed a little while to write a letter to a friend in Buffalo, and then she went out buying with Mr. Pewbrace in his wagon. Once they were done at the stores, they were going to call on some friends of Mr. Johnson. So everybody was out of the house excepting Mr. Otis and me, and before nine he was gone too, calling on some sick people he had been told about the night before. "You have to be a faithful pastor from the first day," he said, which is surely true. I decided to walk around and discover the town. I had it in mind that I might see Mr. Nowac somewhere, and that if I saw him I would ask him if he knew anything about Hanna. I was curious about why he had left the service on the boat when Mr. Otis started talking about her in his sermon. I didn't see him for the reason, as I found out later, that he was already on the road to the Council Bluffs. More than likely I would have been too timid to talk to him anyway.

You can see pretty much the whole of Saint Joseph in about an hour and a half, even if you are not in too much of a hurry. The last place I went to was the docks. The *Jeremy Hadden* had come in the night before, and I walked it off. It is in every way the slickest and best-looking riverboat I have ever seen, and not just on account of it being new. Clayton and I saw it first in Saint Louis, and it was the boat Clayton wanted to take passage on, except naturally we had to go on the *Jane Sure* with Aunt Eusie and Mr. Otis.

Next to the gangway there was a mail wagon with a man watching over it, and there was mail in the *M* box and the *O* box both. Clayton had a thick letter from Clemmy that I had to pay three-cents postage due on, and Aunt Eusie had a packet from Buffalo. The man would not let me take the packet because it was property. Most of the time I am not bold with strangers, no matter their age, but I wanted to save Aunt Eusie trouble, so I began an expostulation with him.

"Miss Otis and I are traveling together. We're staying

for a while at the Presbyterian parsonage with the Reverend Mr. Otis," I said, but he just shook his head. I could not pick up someone else's property no matter where I lived, he told me, even if I signed for it.

"But you let me get the letter," I said, "and that's property, and I didn't even have to sign for that."

"A letter don't have any money value," he said, "except when it's deeds or bonds inside, and then it don't go to anybody except the owner, unless he's dead, and then it goes to his heirs and assigns."

"What about a poem?"

He shook his head. "That ain't got no value."

"What if it's a poem written for pay?" I said to him.

"That letter in your hand got a poem in it that's been bought and paid for?"

"No, but it's maybe got a poem in it that's worth money," I said. "If I can't have the packet, maybe you shouldn't let me have the letter either."

"Could you sell it?"

"What?"

"The poem in the letter."

"To my brother I could. In fact, he would buy the letter even with no poem in it. What I really want to have is that packet so I can save my aunt trouble."

"Could you sell it to a newspaper? I mean the letter. Could you sell it?"

"With the poem in it or without it?"

"Either way."

"Not to anybody with good sense," I said.

"All the same," he said, "I'm going to take it back. You

78

can get your three-cents postage from your brother. It's already after noon and that's closing time. It's against the law for me to pay out money after closing time."

I gave him the letter back and went to a store to see if there was anything I needed to buy. I had money, nine dollars and some change in my pocket, and a ten-dollar piece drove in under my heel, but it was only vanity and idleness that made me want to spend it. Around this time it started to rain, so I went back to the parsonage, ate some bread and bacon, built up the fires downstairs, and started in to reading *Henry the Eighth,* which is not as good as the other history plays, I don't think, but naturally I didn't want to leave it out of my program.

I must have been tired because I fell asleep next to the fire and I was still there when Aunt Eusie woke me up in the middle of the afternoon. It was raining hard and the wind was blowing. I told her right away about the packet, and she and Clayton went down to the dock in Mr. Pewbrace's wagon. I wanted to go along, but Mr. Otis gave me a cup of putty and asked me to inspect the house inside and see after window leaks.

Aunt Eusie's packet was a book of poems about the seasons, sent for her wedding by a friend in Buffalo. Naturally Clayton did not show me Clemmy's letter, but in with it there was a piece cut out of the *Saint Louis Republican,* and Clayton showed me that. It was a story about a fat lady from a circus in Newark, New Jersey. This lady was put on the boards as the fattest lady in the world, over eight hundred pounds, but somebody found out that she was stuffing her clothes all over and did not really weigh but only four hundred pounds, so she lost her job. Clemmy had written "HA HA HA" across the top of the piece and made a drawing of a fat lady and written "CAROLINE" across her bosom.

"I'm going to write her a letter of proposal before the sun goes down," Clayton said.

"Who?" I asked him.

"Clytemnestra," he said.

"Why?"

"Because you have to strike while the iron is hot."

"You mean that newspaper piece? That looks like a more or less cold iron to me, just reading it once."

"You didn't see what was in her letter," Clayton said, "and he who hesitates is lost."

"Haste makes waste," I said, "and he who laughs last laughs best, and all that glitters is not gold."

Clayton smiled and put his finger up next to his right eye. "Chance is the lover's demon, Henry. You remember it was me told you that, and when you get older you'll understand it."

"A promise never made is a promise never broken," I said, "and there's safety in numbers."

For a minute it looked to me like Clayton might think about that, but then he just shook his head. "Words is one thing and deeds is another," he said. "You have to strike while the iron is hot. I'll show you how true that is right now, in case you don't believe it. I bought a horse today. I could tell she was the right horse for me the second I laid eyes on her. Her name is Cassandra and she's pure white. She's no good on farms, the man said, but she's got wind, I tried her on that, and a good disposition."

He took me out to the barn behind the parsonage and showed her to me. She was truly beautiful. The trouble was, I was still more or less exercised thinking about him marrying Clemmy, so I did not pay him too much mind while he was showing me around the horse's features. Any girl who would point out a likeness between her own sister and a fat woman in a circus in New Jersey is nobody to marry. But Clayton, of course, did not see it that way. There is a saying in *Henry the Eighth* that the juice of reason cannot put out the fire of passion, and that is surely true. Along with the horse he had bought a rifle and shot and a hat and a box of trinkets for the Indians, and he showed me the trinkets after we went back to the house. There were a lot of them, mirrors and necklaces and so forth, and he showed them to me one by one. That made me remember Aunt Eusie's wedding and I asked Clayton what he thought we should buy her as a wedding present.

"You want to talk about cold irons," he said, "you can talk about her, fifty years old and getting married with a wedding gown and everything."

"Everybody gets married in a white dress," I said, "except men, of course."

He just shook his head. "She's half a century old, that woman. She was born in 1798."

"That's not so old," I said, "and her Intended is somewhat younger than that."

"I don't want to talk about it," he said. "I have to write my letter."

81

I wanted to keep Clayton from doing that as long as I could. "Just make sure you tell her how you might some day go to China," I said.

Clayton looked at me like this was a new idea to him, which it more than likely was. "What makes you think I might do that?" he said. "I never told you I was going to China."

"It might likely happen," I said. "The Reverend Mr. Sweetvarnish talks all the time about China being a vineyard that needs laborers."

"About as likely as a toad, that's how likely it is. Why should I leave Missouri?"

"You might," I said, "and if you tell her now at the start, she can't complain if you do it. Suit yourself, Clayton. I have no right in the matter."

He shook his head. "I just know I'm never going to China," he said.

"Then you got no trouble and you don't need to pay me any mind at all," I said. "You just write her and say, 'Dear Clemmy, I am going to be a preacher, but don't worry because I will never go to China or any place too far from our people. Please marry me after I finish my schooling, and we will live a long and happy life together close to home.'"

"That's too short," he said. "But now that I think about it, I guess I could put in something about China, or maybe France. That way, whatever I did later she'd have no reason to complain about it. It could save me a lot of trouble."

"There are two kinds of girls in this world, Clayton,"

I said, "the kind who will go to China with a man and the kind who will not go to China with a man."

Clayton went into the parlor right away and wrote her. Naturally he wrote another letter to Mr. and Mrs. Burke telling them of his intentions, and one to our father and mother. When he was done, he went right to bed.

It stopped raining during the night, turning cold, so the next morning the puddles were frozen over, but as soon as the sun was out the ice melted. While I was eating breakfast, I wrote some lines home. I did not in any way want to go back to Saint Louis, but the letter made me sad just the same. I don't remember what I said.

Kanesville and the Council Bluffs are northwest from Saint Joseph, but we started out going straight north to Savannah, which is fourteen miles, because the best road goes that way. It's farm country all that stretch, with the main crop hemp. Savannah looks all right from far off, but it's pretty much of a hole when you get into it. It was the only place that I saw mud in the whole day. Part of the way going there we sang hymns and soldier songs, and twice near Savannah big flocks of finches, hundreds of birds each time, went with us, flying ahead and then waiting for us to catch up and then flying ahead again. Mr. Pewbrace had two strong mules, a little bigger than most, and they walked very fast.

Clayton rode Cassandra back and forth, more or less showing her off, which he had a right to do because she was a fine horse. Mr. Pewbrace spent a lot of time on his horse, Curious, and I drove the mules more than anything else. For an hour in the morning and two hours in the afternoon Aunt Eusie walked next to the wagon. Now, for the first time, I felt like I was really close to the frontier and going some place, and I think Clayton did too. For no good reason at all I got the idea that if we just kept going we would surely find Hanna somewhere up ahead of us.

We got our supper five miles past Savannah at a farm belonging to Mr. Asa Terhune. It's a fine place worth twenty dollars an acre now, he says, and I don't doubt it. His house runs true north and south. He laid it out himself with two sticks by the North Star. From there we turned a little to the west through Holt County. We planned to stay the night on the Coke Hill, but the mules had never walked so far in one day before and they were tired, so we camped in the middle of a grove with a quick spring in it. We were almost thirty-five miles from Saint Joseph.

Clayton is a crack shot, and he has been ever since he was seven. The first morning on our way he got up before anyone else and rode into a gully and shot practice for a while. By the time he came back the rest of us were up and Mr. Pewbrace was making a French breakfast for everybody, which is what he did every morning from Saint Joseph to Kanesville. Clayton was walking, and right away he asked us where Cassandra was.

Nobody had seen her. "Didn't you take her with you?" Aunt Eusie said.

"Not all the way," Clayton said. "I didn't want to shoot near her until she's more used to me, so I tied her a little ways away. Then when I got back she was gone. She should have come here."

"She can't be far," Mr. Pewbrace said. "We'll have some breakfast and trail after her."

"I couldn't swallow a bite of food with my horse lost," Clayton said.

Curious was finished eating, more or less, so Mr. Pewbrace told Clayton that he could take him. "If I was chasing her, I'd go back the road we came. It's the way she remembers, and the wind is blowing from there. It may be she smells something she likes."

So Clayton took Curious off, and as soon as the rest of us were done with breakfast we followed him. The place we all ended up at was a farm about three miles back. Cassandra was in the pigpen rolling around on her back in the muck and looking happy. All at once we knew why the man who sold her had told Clayton that she was no good for farming. When Cassandra saw us she stood up and went back and leaned against the barn, which was the back side of the pen, and nodded at the hogs more or less like they were brothers and sisters.

The farmer was watching both her and us from one corner, but he didn't seem to mind what he saw too much. The pen was on a slope with the mud mostly in the low part and the gate right next to the barn wall, so you could walk in it without mucking up your shoes. Clayton went in and led her out and tied her to the back

85

of Mr. Pewbrace's wagon and begged the farmer's pardon. "I don't mind one bit," he said. "It'll give me something to think about this coming winter."

My cousin John, who knows about such matters, says that a clean pig doesn't smell any worse than a clean dog does, and maybe better. But, naturally, pigs in a pigpen get gamy and stay that way winter and summer, so the truth is that Cassandra stank. Clayton said that we could not give her a bath with so much of a chill in the air, and I believe he was right. "We have to wait until she dries off and then brush the dirt out of her with a brush," Clayton said. We didn't have a brush, but we figured the muck would not dry on her until suppertime, and wherever we stopped to eat we could maybe borrow one.

If the horse had not of been white, I don't think Clayton would have brooded over her like he did. He would have been angry at the man who sold her to him, but he'd of never gotten so thoughtful. "It's like the demons in the hogs in the Bible that run off the cliff," he said. "Hog demons can get in your soul's marrow and persuade you to anything. This one has got my mare believing in her heart that she's a legal certain hog. She's possessed, plain and simple."

"Maybe she grew up on a farm with hogs and doesn't know any better," I said.

"Don't talk foolish, Henry, every horse grows up with hogs, except city horses," Clayton said, which was true. He turned around and looked at her hard in the eye. "She's got a demon, and it has got to be exorcised out of her. Demons always attack the pure ones. They can't abide white. It's a fact. I'm going to exorcise that horse the same way the Reverend Mr. Sweetvarnish exorcised his cow."

It worried me some, him going the whole hog that way all at once, but it didn't seem to worry Mr. Pewbrace at all. He just asked if he could watch Clayton when he did it.

"Sure," Clayton said, "once I piece it all up together. The Reverend Mr. Sweetvarnish had to do the same thing last fall. His cow was possessed and wouldn't give but maybe a pint of milk a day. He got the demon out of her at sunrise, took her to market, and by three o'clock the same day he had her sold."

"A double blessing," Mr. Pewbrace said.

"That's right," Clayton said. "The way Mr. Sweetvarnish says it, sometimes the Lord just gives it out to you with both fists at the same time. The secret is you have to talk directly to the demon and tell him you know he's in there and tell him he has to come out right away. You have to talk loud, and another thing you have to do is prepare the animal ahead. It can't be dirty when you exorcise it. Demons like dirt. And you have to look it in the eye all the while. There's more to it than that, of course, but that's the heart of it, and if you do those things right you get the animal clean."

There was a good steady wind blowing, and the sun stayed out, so Cassandra was pretty much dry by the middle of the afternoon. We stopped and ate a long meal at the farm of Mr. and Mrs. Butz. We could see the Missouri River from their front door, which was the first time that day. Mr. Butz had some stiff brushes and we took an hour to brush down Cassandra. The hardest part was the tail, which Aunt Eusie did, but when we were all done the horse looked as good, or maybe better, than she did the day she was bought. "We probably brushed the demon out of her," Mr. Pewbrace said, but Clayton shook his head. "Demons don't come out as easy as all that." Mr. Butz kept pigs, too, forty or more in a big pen, but we had Cassandra tied up on the far side of the barn, and it was there we brushed her. She kept more or less still except for sniffing the air and tugging at her rope once in a while.

Once Cassandra was clean and the mules were rested, we started on again as fast as we could and only stopped just before dark. We were about sixty miles away from Saint Joseph, and it was Friday, the twelfth of May. Clayton's plan was to do the exorcising the next morning, but he did not tell anybody because he did not want to take a chance that the demon might hear him say it. Before dawn we took Cassandra up to the top of a hill and stood her with her head facing east in front of a big rock, all the while singing hymns, and with Clayton holding a branch of hemlock over her head. If we looked foolish, which I believe we did, at least we sounded more or less orderly. Clayton was *born* a singer, and that's all there is to it.

When it started to get bright, Clayton told Aunt Eusie to stand back a little to the side because once he spoke to it the demon would more than likely come flying out of the animal's mouth and burrow into the first creature it hit, especially if that creature was female, the same as his horse was. "I want to fix it so the demon flies into that rock and gets stuck there, if I can," he said.

All this while, Mr. Pewbrace stayed more or less quiet, but now he came around and stood next to Clayton in front of the horse and looked east, too. "Some people believe one thing and some people believe another," he said after a little bit. "In this present matter, for example, you are a strong and true believer in pig demons, and I must confess myself to be a complete unbeliever."

"Well, like I always say," Clayton said, "every man to his own way."

"The joy," Mr. Pewbrace said, "is when different men of different views work together."

"I suppose so," Clayton said. He was bent forward looking for the sun to come up, and I guess I was bent forward too, because I was curious about what was going to happen next. We were all of us more or less anxious except Mr. Pewbrace.

"There is the call of reason, and there is the call of feeling," he said, "and they need to work together, like partners, so I propose that while you are accomplishing your magic up at the front of this beautiful animal, gazing into her eyes and giving commands that are filled with deep feeling, I stand next to her and speak sweet reason in her ear. How does that seem to you?"

"It can't do any harm," Clayton said.

A minute later the corner of the sun came up and Clayton looked hard at Cassandra, still holding his hemlock branch, and began to talk to the demon, using the same words over and over again, said louder each time. "Demon, get thee gone out of ye white horse here present. Amen." At the same time Mr. Pewbrace, with his arm laid over Cassandra's neck, began talking to her like the two of them were old friends. "Cassandra, my dear, into the life of each creature that God has made there comes a moment when it is time to either spit out the pig or keep him inside. Be sensible, old comrade, assert your true horseness, and do the right thing."

Clayton and Mr. Pewbrace both kept talking on until the sun was all the way up, and then Clayton turned around fast and covered the rock with the hemlock branch and said we should sing all five verses of *Horeb, My Refuge* right away. We did, and after that we went back down the hill again, Clayton in front leading Cassandra.

"I hope you won't take this amiss, Clayton," Mr. Pewbrace said when we were on the road again, "but I made your horse a promise while I was talking to her. I told her I was going to get her a pigskin feedbag."

"That's fine with me," Clayton said. "It could be symbolical of drawing the demon out of her."

This was the first I found out that Clayton believed the demon was gone, which I was glad to hear. We didn't talk about demons for the rest of that day. We crossed the Nodaway River around six, and then stopped for the night. After dinner Mr. Pewbrace, who had on his orange-colored Chinese pajamas with the long red robe and was smoking his pipe, which he always did at night, began talking to Clayton about demon possession.

"Take the case of Cassandra and the pig demon," he said. "How do you know who is doing the possessing? Does the demon of pigness have a hold of the horse, or does the horse have a hold of the spirit of pigness?"

"What sense would there be in that?" Clayton said. "Why would a horse want to keep a demon? That's no kind of company."

Mr. Pewbrace shrugged his shoulders. "People who chew tobacco say it has a hold on them," he said. "As it happens, the heart of chewing tobacco is spitting it out and a chewer can do that any time he wants, so it looks to me as if the chewer possesses the tobacco about as much as the tobacco possesses the chewer."

Clayton hated tobacco as much as he hated demons, and probably more. "Tobacco is a demon weed, all right," he said. "Nobody would dispute that."

"Or take the case of a white person growing up among the Indians, such as the girl Mr. Otis described in his sermon. Do the Indians possess her, or does she possess them, or do they possess each other?"

"The Indians possess her," Clayton said. "It can't be any other way."

"Do you think Indians are demons?" Mr. Pewbrace said.

"I don't know," Clayton said. "I never thought about it."

Mr. Pewbrace stood up to go over to the wagon, where he was sleeping. "Clayton," he said, "we must continue to study life together."

The next day we met Mr. Johnson, and the matter of demons went out of everybody's mind.

⟦ *Chapter VII* ⟧

W^{E MET MR. JOHNSON} late on Sunday afternoon, May 14, when we were still a day and a half from Kanesville. He was on his way with half a load of hides toward Saint Joseph, looking to meet Aunt Eusie on the way. If he did not meet her he was going to sell his hides and move into the Mansion House with Mr. Pewbrace and wait until she came. There was only one good road between Kanesville and Saint Joseph, so he knew he could not miss her.

The land is board-flat where we met, and the road is straight, so we saw Mr. Johnson two miles or more away, and he saw us. He knew what Mr. Pewbrace's wagon looked like from the days when they did trade together, so he stopped and drew his horses around and waited for us. He was short and dark like our uncle who died, Mr. John Case, but where Uncle John was more of a mover, Mr. Johnson was more of a waiter, which is the chief difference between farmers and trappers. He was not a trapper at the time, being then altogether in the trade end of the business, but he had trapped for twenty-five years, starting when he was fifteen, so waiting was in his character.

Aunt Eusie and Mr. Pewbrace and I got down off our wagon, Clayton got down off Cassandra, Mr. Johnson came over, and Mr. Pewbrace did the courtesies between us. Aunt Eusie and Mr. Johnson asked after one another's health, as if they were more or less friendly strangers, and he also asked her about her journey, which she told him was very pleasant. He said he hoped that she would not miss her friends and acquaintances from Buffalo too much during her first little while in Kanesville, and she told him how much she was looking forward to living in Iowa, which his book of drawings had made her ready to do.

When we got started again, Mr. Johnson invited Aunt Eusie and Mr. Pewbrace to ride in his wagon, and I drove Mr. Pewbrace's wagon behind. It was turning cold, and I thought it might snow. Mr. Johnson wanted us to spend the night at Bellevue, on the other side of the river, so we drove as fast as we could to get to the Louse Point ferry before dark.

Following along behind, I got a coltish fancy about Aunt Eusie and Mr. Johnson. I believed that they were going to run away after everybody was asleep that night and get married. I did not fancy this because of anything I heard them say, and with Mr. Pewbrace sitting between them in the wagon they could not even look at each other, so I had no reason for my fancy at all, and naturally it turned out to be wrong.

To get my mind on something real I made myself think about my lie, and I delivered to myself a lecture about how evil I was to tell it. I spoke to myself in strong words, reminding myself that it was my lie about Hanna that had put Clayton and me on this road, him on Cassandra and me in Mr. Pewbrace's wagon, chasing along toward places and people we had not seen before, Clayton all the while carrying a loaded rifle. It came to me that I would not be so hardhearted and shameless about it if I confessed my lie, and I resolved to do that, to either Mr. Pewbrace, or Mr. Johnson, or both of them, the first chance I got. It did not come to me, at the time, that I should confess to Clayton.

We got to Louse Point just before dark and crossed the river to Bellevue. Mr. Johnson was happy because he wanted Aunt Eusie to meet the Reverend Mr. Edward McKinney, who was going to marry them. The Bellevue post is owned by a very generous man, Mr. Pierre Abadie Sarpie. It has been where it is for fourteen years, and it is now a genuine crossroads and platted out to become a town.

Mr. Sarpie sent an Indian boy running to fetch the Reverend Mr. McKinney, and when he came we had a more or less formal supper in the front room of Mr. Sarpie's house, with elk meat, which was very tasty. Six Otoe Indians ate with us, sitting on the floor. One of them was a chief, and he made a speech in honor of Aunt Eusie and gave her a gift, a necklace made out of nuts carved in the shape of bird nests. It was more or less odd to me, eating at a table when there were grown men sitting around on the floor, but nobody paid it any mind, and after a while I did not pay it much mind, either. The chief's speech sounded very musical.

The Otoes have the same words for a lot of different things, and what a word means can depend on if you say it in a high voice or a low voice.

After dinner Clayton said we should write a letter back to Mr. Otis in Saint Joseph telling him that we were all safe together and thinking about him. Clayton had carried a broad bone pen point and a bottle of contract ink with him from Saint Louis, and he was on his way to becoming a serious letter-writer. He took out a piece of his own paper and wrote the first lines, and then the letter went around the circle, ending up with Mr. Johnson. He did not write anything, but he drew a picture of us in a circle around the table, and then we all signed it.

The Reverend Mr. McKinney left a little while after supper, and Aunt Eusie and Mr. Johnson took a walk down to the river, and the rest of us went to bed. Mr. Johnson and Clayton and I were sleeping in the barn loft. Mr. Johnson wanted not to sleep in the same house as Aunt Eusie until after they were married, and the barn was convenient to Clayton because he wanted to be near his horse, and I did not care one way or the other where I slept. Clayton was going to take me out shooting the next morning with him, so we bedded down at the east end of the barn where the sunrise would wake us up.

Once we were lying down, Clayton asked me if I stood with him or not on the question of Aunt Eusie's wedding. "If the both of us feel the same way," he said, "we can go to her and lay out a case. A bird in the hand is worth two in the bush." I did not understand what he meant.

He said that he was against them getting married, and I thought at first it was because they were cousins. This, however, was not the hindrance, as he saw it. He thought that they were too old. "They could live together like brother and sister anywhere they wanted, and nobody to say nay to them. I'm telling you the truth, Henry, the Bible is not strongly for such pairings and yokings as that."

"Maybe he wants a wife," I said.

He shook his head. "It's a worldly thing to do, not to say a fleshly. There's no need when you're both fifty years old to begin a thing like that. They could live together like brother and sister and make out their wills to one another and live convenient and modest with nobody to speak a word against them."

"I don't know that Aunt Eusie is fifty yet," I said, "and he's another three or maybe four years younger than she is."

"That only makes it worse," Clayton said. "It's sinful."

This was a strong opinion, and Clayton had a right to hold it, and I told him so. His notion, however, was that somebody had a duty to speak out, and I should be the one.

"Even savages don't do things like that, marry when they're too old, and for no reason," he said. "It's your duty to tell her that, Henry, because you know her better than I do. Take that Indian from the boat, his brother died and left a big family of women, but he

96

didn't think he had to marry any one of them. That Nowac, I mean. He knew he could do his duty without doing that, and he's nothing but a pagan savage. There are people we know right now that could learn one or two things from him, even if he is nothing but an Indian."

"I didn't know about his family," I said. "In fact, I never knew anything about him at all."

"You never spoke a truer word in your life than that, Henry," he said. "I could tell you things that would keep you up all night."

After he said this he was quiet, almost as if he had fallen asleep, except I knew he had not.

One of the strong points of Clayton's character is that he can keep things to himself. I have no character that way at all. If I had been Clayton, and if I had found out that there was maybe a white girl among Mr. Nowac's relations, I could not have been on the road for four days without telling somebody about it. I asked him, and in fact I begged him, to tell me what more he knew, and after a while he did.

He had come upon Mr. Nowac's French companion, Mr. Couteaux, at Halley's Stable in Saint Joseph. They were both buying horses. When they were done Clayton had asked him about white children brought up by Indians, and he had told about Mr. Nowac's case. Among Mr. Nowac's nieces was a certain girl who looked different from the rest.

"Nobody pays her any too much mind," Clayton said, "because his family gives it out that she's half French

97

on her mother's side. Naturally, nobody cares one way or another about half-breeds, especially where the mother is the white half."

"If she's half Indian and half white she can't be Hanna," I said.

Clayton sat up. "You believe what an Indian gives out, Henry, I guess you'll believe anything."

"Mr. Couteaux believes it," I said. "Besides, I never had an Indian lie to me. I'm more likely to lie than an Indian, probably. That story I told you about meeting that Indian on Chouteau Street and hearing him tell me about the redheaded white girl was a lie."

Clayton didn't say anything for a while. He just lay back down and cracked his knuckles one by one.

"I wanted to get your mind off Caroline's undergarments," I said. "That's why I lied."

"I never thought two minutes together about her undergarments," he said. "She can pad herself out until she looks like that fat woman in the circus for all I care. You know what this means, don't you, Henry? It means that whatever happens on this whole trip is going to lay right on your doorstep, and if things go wrong you're to blame, that's what it means."

He rolled over right away and went to sleep. I went to sleep too, but I woke up in the middle of the night. It was windy outside and there were bits of ice blowing up against the side of the barn. Mr. Johnson was sitting against the far wall. He had a heavy piece of paper on his knees, and a lantern next to him, and he was drawing pictures of Aunt Eusie's face, looking left and looking right, turned this way and that. He drew her the same way he drew all his pictures, with sharp lines showing all her features, and not trying to make her look better than she did in life. There were ten or a dozen pictures in different places on the paper, and it was not something such as I thought he wanted to frame, so I asked him if I could have one of his pictures when he was done. He bent up the bottom part of the paper, which had three heads on it, and cut it off with a knife and gave the piece to me. I took it for a treasure and went back to sleep well satisfied. I still have it.

〖 *Chapter VIII* 〗

THE NEXT MORNING Clayton woke me up early to go shooting. He was very friendly. "I stayed awake all night thinking about your confession," he said after we got down to the river, "and I forgive you for your lie because it was a sent lie, Henry. It was the beginning of a call, you might say, to rescue our cousin Hanna out of her captivity and to punish the heathens who stole her from the bosom of her family. Are you making sure your rifle stays clean?"

"I keep it in oilskin all the time," I said.

"Do you practice with it much?"

"Only when I'm with you."

"Take it to our cousin John's farm when you go and practice more out there. I've shown you all I know about rifles. The rest is up to you. I have a plan. It isn't too hard, if you just do what you're supposed to do, which is what I'll tell you. First, number one, all Indians are afraid of the dark, we know that."

"I don't know that," I said.

"They're savages, and all savages are afraid of the dark. It's a plain, known fact."

"Mr. Nowac is an Indian, and as far as I can tell he probably likes the dark."

"Indians think that there are evil spirits out there, especially when they're living among their own kind," he said. "It's a known fact, Henry, and there's no use in you telling me any different. What's true is true, do you agree to that?"

"To what?"

"To true being true. That true is true."

"I guess I always have believed that," I said.

"All right then. Now, most Indians, I don't say all Indians but most Indians, live in tepees, which are built out of either animal skins or bark. You, being smaller and lighter than I am, you can crawl in under the edge of a tent or a tepee easier than I can, which is what you're going to need to do when the time to rescue her comes, which will be at night. And maybe we'll put a mask on your face. That way they'll think you're an evil spirit if they see you, which there's no reason why they should, and run away, except Hanna, who won't because she's white."

He gave me his gun to hold and got a stick and started drawing on the ground. "Let's say you have twenty tepees in a bunch, which is a more or less sound figure. You just go down in the middle of a dark night and get next to the tepee you believe she's in and find a corner that's loose. Do you think you can do that? You don't think that's too hard, do you?"

"I guess that's pretty simple," I said.

"It's the same thing you did in Caroline's room when you looked in her chifforobe."

"Except there were no Indians in her house," I said.

"Which was a wrong thing for you to do, looking in

her chifforobe, I mean. I have to say that, Henry, now that it's been brought up. It was wrong, going in there and opening drawers and looking into somebody's private property like that. You should feel bad about that, and I hope you do. Anyway, when you find a loose place around the bottom of the tepee you go under it and make sure our cousin is in there like we suppose. If you don't come out right away, it will be a sign to me that you've found her. Then I will begin shooting at tepees in some other part of the bunch. Some of the Indians will run away, and some of them will go to the chief's tepee, and five or six of them will commence to shoot back, which won't matter to you because you will be taking Hanna and running the other way, and it won't matter to me either, because of my long-range rifle."

"I don't know if I can do that," I said.

"Why not?" he said. "It's simple, you said that yourself, and it's bold. I got a feeling in my heart, Henry, that I might could be the Rod of the Lord in this matter, so nothing can go wrong. It's like in the days of old when he called his followers to follow him into the wilderness, even though they knew not the purpose, and yet they were obedient and did go. The Reverend Mr. Sweetvarnish would understand what I'm talking about in a second, and tell me to go right ahead with it."

This speech of Clayton's, instead of resting my mind, made me want to ask Mr. Pewbrace to come along with us. I could not see any profit at all in hunting through strange country in the company of a Rod of the Lord.

We took our time about leaving Bellevue, and still

we got to Kanesville before noon. The town was called Miller's Hollow until three years ago, in honor of Mr. Henry Miller, who started the town and who was a Mormon like most of the other people there. Then they changed the name to Kanesville in honor of Colonel Thomas Kane, who is not a Mormon but who put himself through a lot of trouble to give them credit and protection in their most sore need, as the Bible says it. Now there is talk, Mr. Johnson says, of changing the name to Council Bluffs before some other town does it and takes credit for the countryside around it that way. It is in a flat place with the bluffs on both sides, and when we got there it was just beginning to dry out after a long season of mud.

We ate dinner at Mr. Johnson's house, which has old French furniture in it that he brought down from Canada, and two glass windows in every room, and statues carved into the mantelpiece over the fireplace. Aunt Eusie and Mr. Pewbrace were going to live there alone until the wedding on May 18, a Thursday, with Mr. Johnson boarding out. No place had been fixed up anywhere for Clayton and me to stay in, naturally, and so we were going to spend the first night at Mr. Johnson's house, too.

The next morning I walked out to the Case farm, which is eleven miles northeast from Kanesville on a road that is good for about half the way. Before I left Kanesville I told Mr. Pewbrace about my lie, and about Clayton's belief that Mr. Nowac's niece was really our cousin Hanna, and his intention of going after her to rescue her. Mr. Pewbrace didn't say anything about this, one way or the other. I asked him to tell Mr. Johnson about it if he had the chance, and he said he would.

Two miles from the farm I met our cousin Harold, who was out looking for a hog that had run off. He got down from his horse right away and walked along with me. Harold was the one who was going down to Saint Louis to learn about coopering in my father's shop, and so he was glad to talk to me. What he wanted to know more than anything else was how he would get along with my father. "I know good order and I love good order and I don't have any trouble with it at all," he said after we got in sight of the barn. "What I want to know most is about my Uncle Alvin, your father, and what kind of a boss he is."

I told him that he was a hard boss, but fair, and that he did not like to fire people and hardly ever did it. Harold shook his head and sucked down on his moustache, which he often did, both ends at the same time. "I never once had a bit of trouble with a hard boss," he said. "I work hard and I do my job in a cheerful manner." He got back on his horse and pointed toward the barn. "My brother John's in there. I'm going to go around one more time after that sow before supper. It's not my fault she got away, but I don't mind looking for her, because I do my job with a willing heart. Ask John if that ain't so, if you don't believe me."

So I went to the barn to see John, who is the oldest of our four Case cousins, John, Tom, Harold, and James, who work the farm together. John owns the land and everything on it, so if you were going only by law, the other three brothers are the same as tenants. It is a big fine farm with the best-looking cows I ever saw anywhere, and everybody on it is proud of it.

All four of the brothers look a lot like turtles. The chief turtle feature is the way their heads poke out from their shoulders and slide back and fourth. Turtles are well known to be very canny animals, and they live to ripe old ages, so looking like one is nothing against your character in any way. Still, when you sit at the table with all four brothers for a meal, and they are all chewing and moving their heads around, it is like eating with a family of turtles.

John shook my hand, told me I was welcome, set me to work sorting out seeds with him, which I was glad for, and told me that the work he had in mind for Clayton and me to do after planting was to put a fence around the whole farm, pastures and fields both. "You can build it in your spare time," he said, "and all your cousins will help, inclusive me." He was curious, naturally, why Clayton and I had come already in May, and he asked me if we were going to start work right away. I told him that since Clayton was my elder brother I would leave that business to him, and being an elder brother himself, he was satisfied with my answer. "There's always work enough and more on a farm," he said, "so you can begin any time." All the while he kept looking over my shoulder, expecting that Clayton had come with me and was out hunting the hog with Harold. When I noticed this I explained that Clayton had stayed in town to do some business, and told him all about Aunt Eusie and the wedding. While he was listening to me he kept watching me sorting the seeds, and when I was done he told me that I would soon learn how to sort them faster than I was doing it. "How are my cousin Clayton's hands?" he asked me. "Are they as quick as yours, or quicker?" From the way he talked I could see he wanted us both to be hard at work right away. "I wanted this job to be done by supper," he said, and right after that the supper bell rang and he took me over to the house.

When Hanna was lost or taken, whichever, there were trees close in around the house, but now they're all cleared, and even the barn stands a long way back from it. John is the only one of the brothers married, and he took me in the kitchen the first thing we got to the house and showed me his wife, whose name is Leda. They had been married for only eight months, but she looked like she had been born and grown up in the Case kitchen, or come to it along with the stove, she was so much at home there. She had a small face with little brown eyes, and her features all close together, and she walked back and forth more or less like a beaver, except quicker. She was very friendly, and all the brothers seemed to love her. A stranger, not being told, would probably not be able to guess from watching her which one of the brothers she was married to, or even if she was a sister or hired help. John was very proud of her work. "We had Christmas cake until the middle of February this year," he said, pointing at her. "She does it with water and brown paper in the springhouse." She had many talents as a cook, and she put on a fine big supper that day.

Supper at the Case house is always a long meal, no matter how much work there is left to do for the rest of the day. Right after he prays the blessing, John always tells what work he has already done during the forenoon, and after that everybody else around the table, starting with Tom, does the same. John always knows what everybody is going to say because he lays out the work at breakfast, telling each brother what he is supposed to do. He is fair, and nobody gets less work than anybody else, and he works harder than anybody. Not only that, but he also pokes his head into everything everybody does, and pitches into anybody's work who needs help. That way he sees nearly everything, and it is a rare thing when somebody tells him something he doesn't already know. He likes to see everybody eat a lot, and those who don't eat he gets after with warnings about becoming sickly and dying.

Moral stories and maxims are bread and salt to him, and every Sunday afternoon he writes moral stories for children. He is making up two storybooks for children, and when the first one is done he is going to send it to Boston, which he says is the moral capital of the United States, to be printed and sold. This first book is going to be called *Moral Fables the Red Men Tell,* and the second book is going to be called *More Moral Fables the Red Men Tell.* John hates all Indians, and he would not use a real Indian fable if he knew one, which he does not, but he thinks that children back East will like the idea of reading Indian tales. I asked him if it did not bother him that the title was not true. He shook his head. "Lying to children for their own good is all right," he said. "It's just giving them a dose of their own medicine."

That night he read me some fables out loud to see what I thought. His idea is that children are more or less like sticks of lumber, and the sooner they find this fact out, the quicker they can start changing. "There is nothing in the world more useless and wasted than a child who has got a notion about himself in his head. You have to break a child's will, using iron and honey both, and my books are the honey. It was my mother taught me that, and she knew everything about raising children."

I did not want to argue with his mother's ideas, so I asked him about Hanna.

"My baby sister?" he said.

"I probably should not ask about her," I said, "but you hear stories about white children living with Indians sometimes."

"Hanna? She'd be better off dead than living with savages. Wouldn't you rather be dead than living with savages?"

"I don't think so," I said.

He shook his head. "That's a sign of your ignorance. What if you were a girl? Hanna would be thirteen years old now."

"Fifteen," I said. "She's a year older than I am."

"You wouldn't talk the way you do if you lived in Iowa instead of Missouri. They say people in Missouri are getting soft, and maybe they are, present company excepted."

"I don't know," I said. "It could be."

He shrugged his shoulders. "Well, there you are."

"Even if she was still alive, and I saw her some-where, I probably wouldn't know who she was," I said. "I could walk right by her. She had no special marks a person could tell her by."

"Not true," he said. "She had a wen on her back. She was born with it. And she had red hair."

"But they could dye that black," I said.

"They probably would, too," he said, and then he called them by a profane name.

There was no more to be said about Hanna or the Indians, so I talked about Aunt Eusie's wedding, and said that I was sure he and his wife would be welcome to come, but he said that there was too much work on the farm to have time for social trips into Kanesville.

Clayton came Wednesday night in time for dinner, bringing with him a mule he had rented for me to go north with. She was a good animal, strong and used to riders. Clayton was happy about two things, the bar-gain he had gotten on the mule, only a dollar and a half a week, and the true sinner he had helped to bring to repentance the day before. The sinner was Mr. Hesters-wine, the man who played Maine rummy on the *Jane Sure*. The mule had a good saddle, with a rifle jack and big pockets, so it was really true that Clayton did get a bargain.

John and Clayton hit it off like Clarence and King Edward do at the end of Part Three of *Henry the Sixth,* where the two heroes find each other and go to battle together. Clayton invited him to come into Kanesville for the wedding, and John said he would. He wanted to take Leda with him too, but he said he could not because then nobody would be left home to cook for his brothers. So the next morning after breakfast we set off for Kanesville together. After we got to where the road was open, Clayton asked him questions about Hanna the same way I had, and they got to talking about how much worse than death it would be for a girl to grow up with savages. Clayton told him about Mr. Nowac and how he had stood drinking his coffee in the saloon of the *Jane Sure,* and acting, Clayton said, like it was rum or whiskey and he was a white man. After a while I fell back behind them far enough not to hear. To my shame, I never spoke a word that day in Mr. Nowac's defense. When we were a little way from Kanesville they stopped talking and Clayton started to do rifle practice from the saddle. He said he wanted to get his horse used to the sound and the kick. As soon as we got to town he wrapped up his gun and we went straight to Mr. Johnson's house. It was around noon, and the wedding was at two.

A wedding where the bride and groom are into their far majorities you expect to be of a more or less beefy nature, and full of sobriety and ceremony, like the camp of Pompey the Great as it is described in *King Henry the Fifth,* but it was not that way at all. Aunt Eusie had fixed it for everybody who was coming to march from Mr. Johnson's house to the blockhouse, which required crossing three roads and an alley. We walked on boards that she had paid some boys to lay out so nobody's feet would have to get muddy, and she led the way wearing white silk slippers and with her hair let down, with fresh-picked purple hepatica and wood sorrel sewn onto her apron to cover up the gentian spots. She walked like you would expect a queen to walk, like there was no hurry about anything at all, and people stopped and stood still to see her go by.

I was only at but two weddings before this one, when the Reverend Mr. Sweetvarnish's daughter Elizabeth got married, and when his daughter Mary did the same, and they were sober all the way through. Aunt Eusie's marriage was Frenchified and more like a holiday. There was a *Livre de Mariage* that Mr. Johnson had put together himself, with a border drawn on every page, which everybody had to sign, and there were Indians invited who spoke French and got treated like they were ordinary men.

The sun was bright, which made the blockhouse inside look almost as black as night, even though all three windows in the roof were uncovered and the shutters were down. There were chairs set on both sides, and after the rest of us were in, the Reverend Mr. McKinney marched in carrying his Bible, with Mr. Johnson right behind him, and then Aunt Eusie holding on to the arm of Mr. Pewbrace, who had on a formal suit and was carrying a black cane, waxed and rubbed, with a gold handle.

The vows and scriptures were short, and then Clayton sang a song, and then we all sang a hymn, and then Mr. and Mrs. Johnson kissed each other, and then the congregation crowded outside again. The Reverend Mr. McKinney, Mr. Pewbrace, Clayton, and the bride and groom stayed inside to sign the papers. After a while they all came out, Aunt Eusie first. She looked around for me, but she could not see me right away because it was so bright. After a minute she did see me, and walked over. When she got to me she took my head between her hands and kissed me. "Mr. Pewbrace told me that the first thing I had to do after the papers were signed was to kiss somebody who is both beautiful and good," she said.

It is clear, I am sure, that I am not either beautiful or good, and I confess that recalling what she said to me that day is a vanity, but her words were a blessing to me then, and they still are. Coming into the light out of that dark blockhouse she was like a Jacob's Angel. Mr. Johnson came behind her and asked me to take the *Livre de Mariage* around at the wedding celebration at his house for people to sign, which I did.

It was at the house that I saw Mr. Hesterswine again. He had been at the blockhouse too, he said, but not where I could see him. He had come to Kanesville after going along the river for about a week trying to get a job as a schoolteacher. Not being a Mormon had put him out of any hope, he said. Clayton had met him on the street on Tuesday, and after a meal at Mr. Johnson's he had confessed to Clayton that he was a liar and a cheat.

I felt more or less strange seeing the man, and it could be that he felt a little the same too, seeing me. I watched him talking to Clayton and John while I was carrying the book here and there to be signed. His way of getting what he wanted was to make the people around him proud and careless by telling them that they were better-hearted, or stronger, or smarter than he was, and that he knew it. That's how he won at cards, by acting like a simple man on a streak of luck. He and Clayton and our cousin John sat together on the front porch eating and drinking French coffee. There was whiskey, but none of them drank it. Clayton was talking more than the others, and I thought he might ask Mr. Hesterswine to come hunting for Hanna with us, which to my mind would have been worse than the two of us going alone.

John had brought one of his stories with him as a wedding present, and after a while Mr. Hesterswine got up on the porch rail and hushed the crowd and told them John was going to read it, which he did. The story was called "The Eagle Gets a Wife," and it was about an eagle who hurt his foot. All the animals of the forest came and helped him to do things so he would not have to walk, but none of them did what he needed completely right. Then a lady eagle happened along and nursed his foot until he got better and then he married her. The moral of the story, which was written out at the end so you didn't have to think about it yourself, was that a man should marry his own kind and never lament his infirmities to the public.

After the story the cake and jellies were laid out, and I got Clayton to come into the road with me because he didn't like cake, to talk. At the beginning of *Richard the Second*, the Duke of York says that it is no use carrying good advice to Richard, because good advice always comes vain to his ears. Clayton never had that fault. He does not want to look like a fool, or be one, and he will take good advice if you tell him what you know and don't talk opinions.

"Clayton," I said when I got out on the road, "Mr. Hesterswine is a thief."

"He told me that," Clayton said, "in his past life and right up until the night he almost drowned swimming away from the *Jane Sure*."

"He offered me a ten-dollar gold piece that night if I would lie for him."

"Did you take it?"

"No. He's a cheat and a thief."

Clayton shook his head. "There's nothing you can tell me about him I don't already know."

"That's the way he has of gulling people, Clayton, telling them how bad he is and how good they are."

"Well," Clayton said, "isn't he right? Don't you think I'm better than he is?"

"Yes, I do," I said, "so I don't want him to make you look like a fool, which he could do."

"He tells me he knows this country like the back of his hand and he can smell out Indians in the dark."

"He's a plain liar. I'm a long time liar myself, Clayton, and I can tell."

Clayton got a wondering look on his face. "He says he thinks Mr. Nowac's niece is probably Hanna. In fact, he says he'd be willing to bet money on it, except he doesn't have any."

"How about the money he won at cards?"

"He says he sent it home to his mother, who is a crippled and blind widow. I was just going to ask him to come with us."

"He would be the ruin of anything we did, Clayton, I know he would. And if we do find Hanna, which I am bound to say I do not think we will, and he goes with us, he is going to find a way to take the glory for it. He's got you gulled already, Clayton."

Clayton didn't say anything for a minute, but I could tell he was hot. "I don't know where you get the call to talk about liars, Henry," he said. "He's confessed everything he's done."

"I confessed too," I said, "but with me it wasn't any profit I was after, or glory either."

Clayton got a serious look on his face, and then he took a tin of snuff powder out of his pocket, which I didn't even know he had, and sniffed a pinch of it up each side of his nose. "I hate all forms of tobacco," he said, "but you have to have some acquaintance with the devil in order to fight him. Clemmy told me that, and I think she's right."

I didn't want to argue with him about Clemmy's ideas, so I didn't say anything, and he closed the tin and put it back in his pocket. Then he nodded his head. "We'll just the two of us go after her and nobody else. Did it look like I did that right? The snuff, I mean, did I take it the way you see men do?"

"It looked the right way to me," I said, and we went back in the house.

After telling him that only two of us should go, there was no way I could ask Mr. Pewbrace to come with us, so it was fixed that we would chase after Hanna alone.

⟦ *Chapter IX* ⟧

BEFORE WE WENT TO SLEEP on the night of Aunt Eusie's wedding, Clayton talked to me for a long time about what he wanted to do. He had three aims. The first aim was to rescue Hanna, the second aim was to find some very evil Indians and shoot them to death, and the third aim was to be the only hero of these actions. The stratagem which he had made up, sending me into one tepee while he shot some other tepees down, was not a one-man stratagem, but that did not bother him because he was going to have the gun. His idea was that you could not be a hero unless you had a gun, though you could be just as big a hero with a bad gun as with a good one.

"But we have to do the first things first," he said. "I won't have anybody at all to shoot at until we catch up with that Indian friend of yours and find out where he's got Hanna. Once we find them, we strike like lightning."

"Maybe we won't catch up with Mr. Nowac," I said.

"If he's got a family under him as big as that Frenchman says it is," Clayton said, "then he won't be too hard to find."

"What if we find him and Hanna, both, but she doesn't want to come away with us?" I said.

Clayton shook his head. "Hanna's a relation, Henry. If we don't forget her, and if we don't turn our backs on her, she will not forget us or turn her back on us. Only keep it in mind that everything comes out right for the courageous heart. It's a divine law."

Courage, naturally, is a quality of character that it is important to have, no matter what you do, and so it was right for Clayton to bring it up to me. As far as I could see at the time, he had a lot of courage and a lot of zeal, and I did not have any of either. After he went to sleep I sat up and tried to make my courage greater by looking the dangers in the eye and seeing if they were mortal or not.

There were no mortal dangers that I could see in traveling, except being bitten by a snake, which was not likely, or falling off my mule, which was low, or getting lost, or coming down sick, and three of those things were as likely to happen in Kanesville, or on the farm, as out in the wilderness. I could see a big danger in carrying guns and shooting at people who for their parts could shoot back and hit you and kill you, and a bigger danger if Clayton started shooting while we were trying to rescue somebody who did not want to be rescued, but those things were still far off, and they did not make me as much afraid as Clayton's zeal did.

Zeal was the quality that Clayton had in true abundance, and it showed itself in the strength of his many different beliefs. He believed strongly in his long-range

117

Finch rifle, which was the best, and in his aim, if his target stayed still, and in the Lord, whom he was sure was on his side and not on the Indians' side. Deep in his heart he held the American belief about the Indians and the country. To Clayton, the country was property. The Indians were living on it, but since they had never platted it out, and did not hold any deeds to it, they did not have any rightful claim to it. Wherever Clayton walked, if the land was not held by some other white man, he walked on it like it was his own. The Reverend Mr. Sweetvarnish, for one, looks at the country the same way.

My notion is more on the Dakota French side. The Dakota French, who are mostly trappers and traders, see this country as a place to harvest. They don't own any of it, and they never will own any of it, and they don't think the Americans or the Indians do either. To them, it belongs to the animals.

It was Clayton's zeal about our hunt that made me more afraid than anything else. He truly believed that when the time came he would be able to tell good Indians from evil Indians two hundred yards away by moonlight, and that he had the right to shoot the evil ones dead. This belief made me afraid for him and for myself, and also ashamed that I had not tried to talk him out of it.

The next morning Clayton woke me up early so I could go down to the river and practice shooting with him. He wanted to get out of Kanesville before noon, which as it turned out we did not do, so while we were going along the river we made up a list of things to buy, which was nothing more than food, gunpowder, and shot. His idea was for me to talk to Mr. Johnson and Mr. Pewbrace, since I knew them better than he did, and find out the best way to hunt down Mr. Nowac. "If they ask you why we want to find him, tell them that he owes us some money," Clayton said. "Maybe they can draw you some maps to show the way, or maybe they've got some maps already and you can take them or make copies. Do it carefully and don't make any mistakes." There was a lot of mist coming up off the water, so we could hardly see across the river where Clayton had picked out targets, but it cleared off while we were shooting. Even in the mist, Clayton was a sharpshooter.

We didn't talk while we were shooting because Clayton had a rule against it, but on the way back he told over again his plan for saving Hanna, which was the same as before. I asked him if he had made up his mind yet what we would do if she didn't want to come, but he said that my question was too ignorant to answer. "I'll tell you what you can do right now before breakfast in place of thinking up foolishness," he said. "You can write me out a list of rhyme words that I can put in a pledge poem to Clemmy. I'm going to compose it after breakfast while you talk to Mr. Johnson and Mr. Pewbrace and get their maps, and then we can go buy supplies and see after mail and get on our way. And you better take that ten-dollar piece out from under your heel. I may need it."

I went to the loft and wrote down the end words from Shakespeare's Sonnet Eighteen, and Clayton went in the house to visit with Aunt Eusie in the kitchen. He wrote the poem after breakfast. I never saw it, naturally, but he told me he used all but two of the rhymes, and that the poem was hearty enough, which I am sure is true. While he was up in the loft writing, I asked Mr. Johnson and Mr. Pewbrace how to find Mr. Nowac. "Clayton and I want to see him," is all I told them, but they both knew the reason why. Mr. Pewbrace had told Mr. Johnson about our hunt after Hanna, and by now Aunt Eusie knew about it, too.

Mr. Pewbrace offered right away to come along, but I told him about my bargain with Clayton that it would just be the two of us. Aunt Eusie came in from the kitchen, and I told her that Clayton wanted to leave before noon. I did not say anything about his rescue plan because I did not have a right to, but they all three got more or less worried looks on their faces.

"It's a fool's errand," Mr. Pewbrace said. "That girl you're talking about isn't Hanna Case. I saw her two or three years ago at Vermillion. She couldn't speak English for one thing, and for another she didn't look like a turtle, and all the Cases look like turtles. Did you ever notice that?"

"She never did look like one," I said. "She was the only one in the family who didn't."

"I saw her here in Kanesville not a week ago," Mr. Johnson said. "Everyone else in Nowac's family was here, too, probably waiting for him. I didn't say it to you before because I didn't see any help to be had out of it."

"Did you see her close?" I asked him.

"About as far away as the other side of this room. She was wrapping fish. The smoked fish you ate here yesterday she wrapped. The whole clan was here waiting for Mr. Nowac and peddling things, thirty-five or forty people."

I asked him how old she was, and he said she looked about fifteen. "She stands out because everybody else in the clan is either a lot older or a lot younger than she is. She watches over some of the young ones. And of course she stands out because of her red hair."

"Clayton will take that as a sure sign," I said, and to tell the truth, I thought it was pretty much of a sign, too. It made my heart start beating faster.

"I've never seen an Indian with red hair," Mr. Johnson said, "but if she had an Irish-Canadian mother it could be. Her hair is dark red, like rust."

Aunt Eusie looked over at Mr. Johnson and shook her head. "The number of redheaded half-breed girls with Irish-Canadian mothers is, I think, very small," she said.

"No matter," Mr. Pewbrace said. "I still say it is very unlikely that she's Hanna Case. And if she is, her brothers on the farm would never take her back, anyway. I know John wouldn't. What would she do there?"

"We could bring her with us to Saint Louis," I said.

"How do the Indian women who live in Saint Louis occupy their time?" Aunt Eusie asked me. "Do you know any? Do they live happy lives? You could get hurt trying to take her, and Clayton too, which I'm sure he knows."

"Clayton expects me to go with him, and I have to do it," I said. "He has my promise. Did you say that Mr. Nowac was going to Vermillion?"

Mr. Johnson nodded his head. "If he isn't there he's most likely gone north toward the Badlands, and not even your brother will want to follow him up that way," he said. "When does Clayton begin his divinity studies?"

I wasn't sure, but I said I thought he would want to start in October.

"Well then," Mr. Pewbrace said, "I for one will hope and pray that Mr. Nowac has left Vermillion, and that he stays north until the end of September. I don't know if he shoots men or not, though I suppose he would if he had to, but they say he's a crack game hunter."

Mr. Johnson didn't have any maps showing Vermillion, but he told me what sites to look for on the way, and I wrote down a list. I can find my way places more or less directly once I have the sites in order. Aunt Eusie brought some coffee, and when she gave me mine she said she thought it was right for me to go. "You have to keep your promise," she said. "But Clayton is a timid man, and timid men hate to take the blame for anything, so you should do only what you alone are ready to answer for."

I was surprised to hear her say this, but I believed her.

It was almost eleven before Clayton finished his letter with the poem in it. He gave it to me and said that I should take it to the post office right away. "While you do that, I'll see after the buying of what more we need, and we'll meet back here," he said. Mailing his letter,

I also picked up the letter Aunt Eusie wrote to Mr. Johnson the day she bought the boat tickets for the *Jane Sure*. It had arrived in Kanesville that morning.

At the post office I took paper and wrote one letter to Caroline and another one home. It was a social letter I wrote to Caroline, and I did it because I thought I owed her one, since Clemmy was hearing from Clayton all the time. I had seen Caroline in a dream on our first night in Saint Joseph, and in the dream she had come over to me and kissed me on the mouth. I had never had a dream before exactly like that one, and it made me feel as if I should ask Clayton's pardon. I would have, too, except that when I woke up the next morning he was already out shooting, so I never did it. Now I felt as if I should confess to writing the letter, which I did first thing when he came back with the supplies. He just bit off a hangnail and shook his head. "Never give your heart to a false woman," he said.

By then it was suppertime, and Clayton decided that we should stay and eat. He didn't seem to mind or act like he was in a hurry. When we sat down he told Aunt Eusie that we were going to eat a lot and enjoy it because we wouldn't eat this well again until we got back, and when the duck went around for seconds he said the same thing to Mr. Johnson.

"Stay here with us," Mr. Johnson said, "and eat this way every day."

Clayton shook his head and got a sad look on his face. "I can't," he said. "I need to study the ways of the savages, starting with Henry's good friend Mr. Nowac. Did you know, Mr. Johnson, that he helped Henry out the night we rescued your wife's chest from the storeroom of the *Jane Sure?* He held the lantern for him or something."

"He lit it for me and showed me how to get in the storeroom from a trap door in the engine-room wall," I said, "but I didn't help him at all. He had some bolts of silk to rescue."

"I was proud to be Henry's brother that night," Clayton said, and I could tell from the sound of his voice when he said it that he truly believed it. In fact, as far as I can tell, Clayton always believes everything he says at the time that he is saying it.

"Clayton, you should stay right here for at least a month and act as watch and ward over me," Aunt Eusie said. "You can see after my stewardship as a wife, and give me correction when I need it."

"I would honestly like to help," Clayton said, "but to tell you the truth, Mrs. Johnson, I also have a religious reason for going. It might be I could some day receive the call to preach to the Indians, and that puts me in duty bound to prepare myself. I think the Divine Voice may be calling me in that very way this very minute." As he said this he held his fork up in his right hand and sat stock still, like a picture.

"Maybe you'll find your cousin Hanna," Mr. Pewbrace said.

Clayton did not expect Mr. Pewbrace or anybody else to say that. Still, he did not blush, but only looked surprised. Then he tilted his head back and looked at the ceiling, like the Reverend Mr. Sweetvarnish sometimes does. "I fear not," he said. "She was a very fine type of girl, very delicate in her constitution, and not the sort of plant to survive an Indian winter, if you take my meaning."

"Even if she is alive," Mr. Johnson said, "she's not within a thousand miles of here."

Clayton looked down at his plate. "She was very delicate," he said. "May the Lord rest her soul and forgive those who caused her grief, if any did, which it may be so and it may not be so. When I come back here in two weeks I will visit with the Reverend Mr. McKinney, and tell him what I have learned about the savages, and get his counsel and advice about it. Naturally, I may not be called to go among the savage Indians at all. Henry thinks I should preach in Paris, France, or perhaps China."

Clayton then told everything he thought he knew about the heathens in Old Europe, and the need to clean up the sinful cities there. "If you are going to wrestle against the devil, you have to go where he is, and according to our friend the Reverend Mr. Otis, now preaching at the Andrews Church in Saint Joseph, Paris is the worst place of all. It makes my blood boil to think of so much darkness in one place. Pass the duck, please."

When the time came for us to go I was ready, but I was sorry to leave Mr. Johnson and Aunt Eusie and Mr. Pewbrace, because they were all good people and good company. I still owed Mr. and Mrs. Johnson a wedding present.

We started for Vermillion at about two in the afternoon. It was Friday, May 19. Clayton has always been an excellent person with whom to travel. He never tries to eat more than his share, or get a warmer or drier place than you have, and he doesn't complain. If you know the way to go, he lets you take the lead. He likes to see you happy. On long flat stretches, or when the weather keeps you from traveling, he gives lectures and tells stories he has heard that pass the time. He is careful and he is serious-minded. He makes harmless jokes to keep you happy, and he does not overwork his animals. The only worry I had with him between Kanesville and Vermillion was my fear that he would roll over in his sleep one night and shoot himself. He had the barrel of his gun pointed at his feet all the time, which was cautious, but he had a fifty-three grain charge in it, which is enough to take a lot away from you. Whenever I had to get up in the night those six days, I always walked around his head end and never let his feet point at me.

As soon as we got out of Kanesville we had a talk about different kinds of lies, and what makes them bad, and what has a right to be called a lie. Clayton called my lie about Hanna a bad lie, in the first place, because I was deceiving my only brother, but a good lie, in the second place, because it put us hot in pursuit of a relation who was in deep need. It was very rare, he said, for a bad lie to change into a good lie, but that is what had happened with mine. "If you want to know what I think, Henry," he said, "I think it was a sent miracle and nothing less."

He repeated this idea four or five times in one pleasant way and another, and then finally he asked me if I thought he had lied at supper, telling Aunt Eusie and Mr. Johnson and Mr. Pewbrace about his plans and intentions.

"Yes," I said, "I think you did."

"Well, Henry," he said, "then you don't know the truth when you see it. I told the almost complete truth. It is a fact that I want to study the savages. I could be called to preach among them at almost any time, since the Spirit moves where it is listing, like a boat, so I do need to learn about them. Also, it is true, as I said, that Hanna could be dead, and it is true that I could go to Paris, France."

"I don't mind, Clayton, but you did leave out the real reason we're going to Vermillion," I said.

"It may be I left out one reason, Henry, but at least I didn't say that I was going to go into Hanna's tepee and look in her chifforobe and see what she had in there. Do you understand what I'm talking about, Henry?"

I did not need to say anything, because he knew the answer.

"All right," he said. "Then if I tell certain people, people who are not in any way or shape relations or kin or anything else to us, if I tell them that I might go to Paris, France, that's no reason for the pot to call the kettle black, especially when the pot, which is you, Henry, is a lot blacker, and say that I'm lying. I'm not mad at you, Henry, I'm just trying to tell the truth about who is the real champion liar between the two of us."

"I know I'm not truthful, Clayton," I said. "I can't remember all the lies I've told, there are so many."

"I'm glad to hear you say that, Henry," he said, and then as a joke he rode over close to me and kicked my mule, trying to jostle me a little. "Now tell the truth about this one thing. You didn't after all look in Caroline's chifforobe that day, did you? I won't be mad, I just want to know."

"You're right, Clayton," I said. "I didn't look in it."

"I knew that all along. And I'll bet you didn't even go upstairs, either. I was playing the piano and singing, so I couldn't see you."

"If you give me forty-five to one odds, I'll bet ten dollars I did go upstairs," I said, but his mind was so far away from thinking about Aunt Eusie's bet against Captain Fountain that he didn't understand what I meant.

"I'm right, aren't I?" he said.

"I didn't look in her drawers, Clayton, but I did go upstairs," I said. "Prince came up after me. We both knew we shouldn't be there, but there we were, just the same."

Clayton got a sad look on his face. "Shame on you, Henry, trying to blame your sins on a poor old dog with half his hair gone off his back."

"I'm not trying to blame him, I'm just saying he had a bad conscience about it. I think that's a credit to him, dog or not," I said. "And I still think what I told you about her undergarments was true, that they never were stuffed, even though it doesn't make much difference either way."

"I don't think we should drag a lady's name into this,"

Clayton said. "Clemmy was trying to do the right thing when she told me. It was her duty to speak the truth."

We stopped talking about lies, then, and the rest of the afternoon and into the night Clayton talked on and off about Clemmy. He wanted to recite the poem he had written to her, but he could not remember it well enough even after I got out my Shakespeare and read him out the rhymes.

During the next few days we had many more pleasant and instructive talks. If you are traveling to Vermillion from Kanesville, you just keep going for six days in a more or less northwest direction, making sure to climb a tree two or three times a day to see that the Missouri River is still on your left, and you can't get lost. On May 20, we came to a prairie fire that was five or six miles from rim to rim. There was no wind driving it, so we just stamped out the part in front of us and walked through. With a strong wind, Mr. Pewbrace told me once, a prairie fire is a different sort of beast entirely.

The most troublesome part of the journey was getting over Hog Weed Creek, which we did the third day toward night. Hog Weed Creek is about four feet wide and two or three feet deep, but it goes across the prairie in a gully about twenty feet deep, and the sides of the gully are straight up and down, so that there is no way to lead an animal down one side and up the other. We turned right, figuring it would get even deeper near the river, and saucer up the farther we got away. It did not happen that way, however, and by the time we got back to the river, where the banks broke down and we could cross, it was time to stop for the night.

We got to the Vermillion Post on Thursday, May 25. It is on a very low rise about two miles long each way. Most of the prairie in that part of Iowa is about thirty or forty feet above the river, and the Vermillion land is maybe thirty feet higher than that, and more or less flat, with a little crease in the middle where there is a spring. It is the only spring we saw on the whole way from Kanesville, the rest of the water being ponds and bow-shaped lakes.

Upriver of Vermillion is open prairie, but downriver there is a considerable woods that goes all the way to the bank of the Missouri and then takes up again on the other side. When you get through the woods you are less than two miles from the post and you can see the Indian lodges along the south edge of the rise. These are square buildings covered with skins, with corner posts three and four inches thick driven deep into the ground. Inside, the lodges are parceled out into rooms. If you want to move them you strike the skins and braces, but you have to leave the corner posts behind, they being too heavy for trail animals to carry and also too long to be convenient. We saw corner posts sticking up out of the ground on the east side of the Big Sioux River while we were on our way, and the lodges long gone.

We went to the trading post right away and visited with Mr. Pascal Cerré, who keeps it. He told us that three of the lodges were overseen by Mr. Nowac, and that his clan had eighteen or nineteen women and fourteen men in it, plus some children. He knew how many men there were because they all traded with him and each one had a page in his account book, but the women he wasn't so sure of.

Mr. Nowac, he said, had come back to the post on Monday night, bringing his whole clan with him, and we would most likely find him at the bandy plat at the north end of the plateau. Before we left to go there, he asked us to eat buffalo tongue with him and his wife that night. I wondered if his wife was an Indian, but she turned out to be a Swede.

All the Santee Indians play bandy, sometimes a hundred or more on each side. They put a stake in the ground at one place, and then another stake the same size a half a mile away, and then mark the sides with little switches, making the bandy plat more or less square. There is a hide ball which is stuffed full of leather thongs braided in the shape of corkscrews and sewed tight shut. The game is to hit the other side's stake with the ball, and doing it twice wins. After that, if they still want to play some more, they mix up the sides and start again. You can pretty much do any-thing with the ball you want except throw things at it to stop it. You can kick it, or run along holding on to it, or throw it in every direction, or lay on it. Anybody can bump anybody, back or front, except there is no butting allowed. You can have as many people as you want on each side, and anybody can play who wants to, and I think you can even change sides in the middle of the game.

The game wasn't started yet when we walked over,

and I right away saw Mr. Nowac's niece. I did not tell Clayton that I saw her, and he kept looking around for her every which way. I knew her because she had her hair tied back with a strip of silk from one of Mr. Nowac's bolts. It was dark red, and from the way it hung down I figured that the darkness probably came from either brown grease or pitch resin. She was bent over talking to two girls about ten years old, so I didn't see her face. My heart started beating fast. I wanted to talk to her, and I was afraid at the same time.

There was no signal, as far as I could see, but all at once the game was going. For a long while there was just a lot of running this way and that. Nobody got hurt until a man with white hair fell down on the ball and everybody bunched up on him and around him. Two men got knocked silly trying to get the ball loose, and ended up walking around in circles while the game went off somewhere else. The two girls with Mr. Nowac's niece wanted to run out onto the field then, you could see, but she held them back.

It was a small man who put by the first point. He caught the ball when it was aimed at somebody else and ran fast as he could about two hundred yards and then flung himself and the ball together into the pole near us over the heads of the guards. Right after that, Mr. Nowac's niece joined the team that was losing. She just ran out onto the field and waited for the ball to come back our way again. She had on a long skirt, which was hitched up a little way under her belt, and she could run faster than anybody on that prairie.

I did not see her face clearly until she came running

132

back toward our side, chasing after a big man with a fur hat who was coming along the boundary holding the ball out in front of him with both hands. He looked like a bear trying to get home with a hive, all the more that way because the ball had been beaten into more or less of a hive shape by then. Mr. Nowac's niece was running almost alongside of him.

Even with her big skirt on, it was clear that her legs were longer than most. According to my mother, there are three ways girls can look, either pretty, or plain, or common. Nowac's niece looked to me to be plain. At the time, for certain, she did not care how she looked, her whole mind and soul being fixed on keeping the bear away from the goal.

Clayton saw who she was when she and the bear went pounding and thumping by us. Ten running steps farther on, she jumped in front of him feet first, and the two of them fell down and rolled over three or four times. Clayton looked at me and grinned. "That's Hanna," he said.

"If it is," I said, "what will our cousins do with her on the farm?"

〖 *Chapter X* 〗

RIGHT AFTER THE SECOND GOAL was made against her team, which took about an hour, and while everybody was milling around and greeting each other, it came to me that I should go over to Mr. Nowac's niece and talk to her and try to buy her hair ribbon to give to Aunt Eusie as a wedding present. It would not have been a very fine present, and if she had sold it to me I expect I would have kept it for myself, but at the time, buying it for Aunt Eusie looked to me to be a very good idea.

My plan was to ask her who she was, first, and then find out if she would sell me the ribbon, and then see what happened after that. The chief thing, naturally, was to find out who she was, and the best way to do that was to get her to tell me herself, which meant that she would have to remember her name, and remember English, and not be afraid of me.

I told Clayton what I wanted to do, and he acted more or less for it. "Go ahead and do it," he said. "I don't have anything against doing it."

"You want to come with me?" I said.

Clayton shook his head. "It's just as good if I wait for you here. We don't both have to do that. Nobody is going to hurt you in a crowd like this. You don't have to worry."

So I went and found her right away. She was walking with one of the two girls toward the lodges, and not going too fast. When I got close behind her I said "Hanna," loud, in a way that made it sound more like a word than a name. She stopped and turned around, and the little girl with her, too. Her eyes were the same color as Mr. Nowac's, except clear and maybe a little bit larger. "I want to buy a wedding present for my aunt," I said. "She's not really my aunt, but I call her that."

This was not a promising thing to say, and it sounded foolish to me even while I was saying it, but to judge from the look on her face she did not understand what I was saying, anyway. It was like Henry the Fifth talking to Katharine of France before she learned English. She shook her head and turned around and walked away, and I went back to where Clayton was waiting for me. On the way I made up my mind that it was time for me to speak out against his plans for shooting down tepees.

"I should have said this to you before," I told him when I got to him, "but I don't think you should shoot at those lodges, because somebody could get hurt or even killed."

"Don't talk so loud," he said. "Did she answer to her name? Did you use it?"

"I don't think she even knew it was a name," I said.

"Then that proves it's her," he said. "It takes ten years to forget a language, and that's how long Hanna's been gone, almost exactly. And to forget your name you have to start young, when you're about five or six, which is how old she was when she was stolen. Who else could she be?"

To this argument I had no answer, so I brought up his shooting plans again.

He moved his rifle around to the side away from me, to show that he was listening, and put his finger onto his lips. "Never talk about guns in the middle of a crowd of Redmen," he said. So we left and went and sat down on the post porch. "First off, Henry," he said, "I have not been the one of us to talk about hurting people. Not one time have I said anything about killing anybody dead, Indian or otherwise. That's the truth, isn't it, Henry?"

"I don't remember, Clayton," I said, "but every time you talk about shooting, it worries me."

"It's true I could split an owl from two hundred yards away, but that doesn't mean I'm going to do it," he said.

"You've always got it loaded," I said.

"Frontways or sideways, first shot," he said. "Naturally, the bird has to be sitting still. I can't promise anything when it's flying through the air."

"Maybe I'm being foolish, Clayton," I said, "but I am very uneasy in my mind. I know I should have said this to you before."

He held his hand up in the air. "Henry," he said, "I will never shoot an Indian except when I see that he is an agent of darkness abroad in the world doing evil."

"But you might not know for sure what kind of agent

he is from two hundred yards away," I said, "especially if it's at night."

"Or for one other reason," Clayton said, "if he is going to do harm to morals. Any man of honor would do that."

"Does that mean you won't shoot at the lodges?" I asked him.

He didn't say anything for a minute, and then he looked up at the sky. "There's just one thing I want to know, Henry," he said. "When we're finished and people ask who the hero of all this is, what are you going to say?"

"I'm going to say you are, probably," I said, "because it will probably be true."

"Will you feel it in your heart, so people will believe you?" he asked me.

"People always believe me when I say something modest like that," I said. "I don't care too much who the hero is as long as nobody gets shot."

Clayton patted me on the back. "You're young, Henry, or you wouldn't say that," he said.

"Why don't you catch her somewhere and talk to her," I asked him. My notion was that even if she ran away from him, he would have something to tell about.

"You know perfectly well I can't do that, Henry," he said. "She'd take one look at my rifle and run away."

"Don't bring it with you," I said. "I'll watch it for you while you're gone and make sure nothing happens to it."

"And walk around unprotected in a camp full of heathen unbelievers and savages?" he asked.

"Mr. Cerré probably walks around that way all the time, and nothing happens to him," I said.

"He's French, which makes him almost one of them," he said, "and you can walk around safe because you're just a boy and they know you can't hurt them. I'm an altogether different case. I'm white, and besides I'm American, and I'm a man, so they know me for an enemy right off. Clemmy would be against me doing it, too, since it would put me in danger of being alone with another female."

He looked so sad I thought he might cry. He poked the end of his gun into the dirt and started digging a rut with it. I don't remember ever in my life seeing him look so sad. "The worst thing is," he said, "those lodges don't give you anything to shoot at. If they were tepees I could aim at the tops and probably knock a bunch of them down. You'd see those Redmen scamper then. You should have told me, Henry, that they didn't have tepees, when I first drew you out my plan on the ground."

"I didn't know it," I said, "but I should have said how I felt about shooting at them, I confess that, Clayton."

"What are we going to do with the trinkets I went and bought?" he said. "I'm beginning to think I didn't need to do that."

"Did they cost a lot?" I asked him.

He shrugged his shoulders. "Two dollars," he said.

I got an idea that seemed more or less safe. "Why don't you follow along after me the next time I talk to her, and protect me in case somebody attacks me," I said.

138

He took the rifle end out of the dirt and looked at it and started to clean it. "I could use this gun, plus the one I gave you, both," he said. "I want you to see what a sharpshooter your brother really is, Henry."

"I already know," I said.

"I mean in a real need, against a real live standing target," he said, and then he patted me on the back again. "You have good ideas, sometimes, Henry, I have to confess that."

"I want to be a good brother to you, Clayton," I said.

"We have to stick together, Henry," he said.

A little after this, Mr. and Mrs. Cerré called us in off the porch because dinner was ready. They gave us buffalo tongue, a wild duck, three different kinds of spring greens, and bread with gooseberry jam. While we were eating and as long as it was light we watched the Indian lodges through the side windows of their house.

Clayton asked after Mr. Nowac, and Mr. Cerré said he thought he was getting set to go to Canada. All but two of the men in his clan had already justified their accounts, and Mr. Nowac was selling and bartering off his silk for horses and goods he could sell up north. Mrs. Cerré had bought eight yards of it herself for a high price.

"His redhead niece is a great games player," Clayton said.

"Not only that, she's an excellent swimmer, too," Mrs. Cerré said. "I watched her two months ago jump into the river and bring in a loaded canoe that had broken loose."

"They say she had an Indian father and a white mother," Clayton said, "but I don't believe it."

"I don't know anything about that," Mr. Cerré said.

It was dark when we left them. We tried to leave before then, but Mrs. Cerré had two cabinets full of Italian glass to show us, piece by piece, and Mr. Cerré had four boxes of natural objects from the Badlands to show us the same way. He had five petrified turtles of different sizes, one of them completely whole except for a crack in the shell and no eyes, and the petrified head of a small bear, and a lot of skulls with working jaws. He also had the head of a big horned sheep. Mrs. Cerré's glass objects were very beautiful, too.

After we got out we went across to spy on the lodges, but they were more or less quiet so we turned around and went back to the post, where Mr. Cerré had opened up a room for us. After we were in bed I told Clayton about the wen which our cousin John had said was on Hanna's back. It was news to him and he was glad to hear about it. He wanted to know what part of her back it was on, but I couldn't tell him.

"Mr. Nowac's niece could have a wen on her back and still not be Hanna," I said, "because as far as I know, a lot of females have wens."

"Do wens stay on for life?" he said.

"The only thing I know about wens is that in the second part of *Henry the Fourth*, when the King is talking about John Falstaff, he calls him a wen because he can't get rid of him," I said.

"Did you ask John how big it was, or the color or the shape of it or anything?" he said.

"I forgot to," I said.

"You should of asked him, Henry," he said, which was true enough.

We were both quiet for a little while, and I believe I started to fall asleep. "Henry," he said then, "I trust you to do the right thing. I always have and I always will."

"Thank you, Clayton," I said.

"I'm going to fall in with your plan," he said. "You talk to her alone and I'll guard you to see you're not attacked."

"The only trouble is, I don't think she knows any English," I said.

"We can cross that bridge when we come to it," he said. "First things first, which is to get her alone somewhere. Go to sleep, Henry."

The next morning when I woke up, Clayton was already awake and down at the river practicing with both guns. I could tell the difference by sound because my gun carried a smaller charge and had a shorter barrel.

I ate a few biscuits and went over to Mr. Nowac's lodge to find out when he was going north and which lodge his niece was in. On the way there I gave myself courage by telling myself that if she was Hanna she might really want rescuing, and that it was my duty, as Clayton said, not to turn my back on her.

Still, it was somewhat *unmeet* for me to visit Mr. Nowac, and I did not expect to stay long. There were no sorts of debts or obligations between us, or calling habits, and we were not the same race or nation or age.

I got a little girl to point out his lodge and then I just

stood outside the doorway for somebody to see me and tell him I was there. After a while he came out and looked at me. I remembered the *Jane Sure* on the night it sank, and the way he looked coming around the corner with the lantern. I had been afraid of him then, truth to tell, and I was afraid of him now, not that he would do me harm, but that he knew what I wanted and what I was thinking. It was like standing in cold water in the engine room of the *Jane Sure* again.

We shook hands. "She cannot see you," he said.

"Oh," I said, or something like that.

"You did not come to court her," he said.

"No," I said.

"Or your brother."

"We think she might be a relation, a cousin, my aunt and uncle's girl."

"You are here for them?"

"No, they both died."

"She is one of my family," he said. "You cannot see her."

"I admire the way you speak English," I said. It was a foolish thing to say, but it was true and I did not want to talk any more about his niece.

"I know less than three hundred words," he said. "Good day."

He turned around and went inside the lodge, and I started walking back to the room, looking out for Clayton. Before I left, I think I saw her head just inside the entrance, but I'm not sure. On the way I got an idea, and I told it to Clayton as soon as I saw him. "She's a swimmer," I said, "and I'll bet she swims at least one more time before they go north. The best place to swim is where the woods go down to the river. I'll meet her there, and you sit in a tree close by with the guns and act as watch. She'll probably go there either tonight or tomorrow morning, or maybe the next night or morning, depending on when they leave."

"We'll do it," Clayton said. He went right away and told Mrs. Cerré that we were leaving that afternoon to go back to Kanesville, and bought from her some bread and sweet lard to tide us over until we could shoot game or get fish. We left a few hours after supper, went into the woods a little way and tied the horse and mule, and then walked down to the water. Upstream the river bent west, so you could see our shore for about four miles that way. Clayton found a tree near the edge of the woods with a high crook in it, and when the sun started to set he climbed up. On the way he got his belt caught under a knot, and almost tore the buckle loose. It was the belt Clemmy had given him, that her grandfather had worn in the Battle of Saratoga, New York. He took with him two blankets, one to lean back against and the other to wrap himself in, and both rifles, and half the bread. If Mr. Nowac's niece did not come between sundown and sunrise we decided we would meet again under the tree and let the spirit be our guide as to what to do.

The bank of the river was more or less steep. I went with a blanket and sat down right under the edge of the bank so I could watch across the prairie to the post with nothing but my head showing.

There was not much to do, waiting for her, but to

think about things, and in my fancy I took her back to John's farm by horse, and then to Kanesville the same way, and then to Saint Joseph by wagon, and then on the boat back to Saint Louis. The only place I could truly fancy her was in Saint Louis, and may the Lord forgive me for it, the way I saw her was in a coffin with the lid down, like she was a foreigner dead of the cholera.

When my mind was all the way back to Saint Louis I turned it around and remembered the journey to where I was, starting with the lie about Caroline's undergarments, which brought on the lie about meeting the Indian, and led in a more or less straight road to the river and the riverbank and that night.

The moon was up before the sun went down, and the sky was clear. In the first hour after dark the girl did not come, and so I did not expect her until just before morning. I began to nap on and off, knowing that I would be safe until the moon went down at least, which I was. When the moon was going behind the trees across the river I woke myself entirely up and began a steady watch on the prairie between the Indian lodges and me.

She came before sunrise, almost like she had the intention to meet me. She had the two little girls with her, and I could hear them talking, even if it was very softly, when they were still a long way off. The sky in the east was just beginning to get light, but it was still almost as dark as night. Somebody back at the lodges stirred up a fire and then put it out. I wondered if that was a sign of Mr. Nowac's clan getting ready to leave.

The girls came past me not fifteen yards away and went down the bank and started to take off their clothes. All of a sudden I felt like I did that Sunday in Caroline's room, when I wanted to look in her chifforobe and could not do it. I don't know how much I would have seen, since it was almost as dark as night down next to the river. I wanted to peek, anyway, but I knew that it was unjust to look at people from hiding, like a thief, so I looked the other way until I heard them get into the water.

They swam downriver with the current until they were about a hundred yards away, and then turned around. They were starting to swim back up when my gun went off. I turned around and on the prairie, about two hundred and fifty yards away, I saw Mr. Nowac. He was standing still and looking toward the trees. Clayton, I found out later, not wanting to shoot at an old man who was moving, had shot up into the air to scare him away. I knew which tree Clayton was in, but it was still dark in the woods and I couldn't see him. I think I saw the smoke from his shot drifting out of the trees, but I can't be sure because there was some mist, too.

When I turned back the girls were already out of the river a little way downstream and were running along the shore toward where they had come down the bank. I was standing in plain sight on top of the bank, but they didn't see me. Mr. Nowac's niece was running behind them urging them along, and she didn't see me either until she was right below me, and then she looked up. I put my arms out right away to show her I didn't have a gun or a knife or anything. She ran along eight or ten steps farther so as to be between me and the other two girls, and then she turned around and faced me while the girls ran on. She looked mad, and she was a little out of breath, more probably from the scare than the running.

Saint Paul talks about *tongues and the interpreting of tongues* in the First Epistle to the Corinthians, his idea being that sometimes a person can be gifted to understand a language he does not know. Something like that happened with me. She walked a little way toward me, away from the mud and up a little bit into the light, and said something in another language, speaking more or less slowly. She had a serious look on her face, but her voice was sweet and calm, and what I heard her say was, "You came after me, and now you see me," which was true. She deserved to be called a woman, not a girl. She looked very beautiful, and not plain in any way.

The two little girls were pretty far up the river now, and they climbed the bank and started to run toward the post. Mr. Nowac called out to them and started running toward them. Right after that I heard Clayton shoot his own gun, and his niece turned and ran. I didn't see whether she had a wen on her back or not.

Clayton claims that the bullets from his gun travel ten times faster than the noise does, and that could be. I know for a fact, however, that I heard the sound quite a bit before I felt the bullet.

Clayton had not planned, when he went up the tree, to shoot me. His plan had been to wait for some evil

Indian to grab me and hold still long enough to be hit. When Mr. Nowac started running toward the little girls, who were also running, I was the only still target around anywhere. He couldn't see Mr. Nowac's niece, and he would not have shot a woman anyway, cousin or not. He was a sharpshooter, and he had been waiting to shoot somebody all night, and when he aimed at me it was to hit a place where I didn't have any vital organs, in the fleshy part of my right side. The way he saw it, I was the only party he could shoot at, and also the best one because the least harm was meant.

I sat down and Clayton ran over to me as fast as he could. He looked somewhat surprised over what he had done, but naturally he was proud too, because he had hit me right in the spot he had aimed at. He kneeled down beside me and asked me if I could walk back to the post, but I was sure the bullet had cracked a rib, which turned out to be the case, so I told him no. By now some Indians were running toward where we were, men and women both. Four or five of them picked me up and carried me back to the post. Clayton would have helped them carry, but when he stood up his belt buckle broke and his pants fell down.

⟦ *Chapter XI* ⟧

M RS. CERRÉ strapped me up and put me to bed and fed me raw meat, but the rib was never any trouble to me, then or since. After four days she let me get up. By then Mr. Nowac and his clan were three days gone. Clayton saw them leave Vermillion, and even followed them a little way. "Hanna was walking at the end of the line, throwing a leather bag back and forth with a little boy," he said. "She was laughing. I couldn't believe it."

Clayton, of course, never had any proof that the girl really was Hanna, but I believe he was right.

We left Vermillion on June 2, and were back at the Case farm on June 9. Our cousins, and John's wife, Leda, were kind to us all summer, and we learned many things about farming before we returned to Saint Louis. Looking back on that whole time from early May to the end of September, I do not regret anything that happened except the sinking of the *Jane Sure,* which was a dead loss. I became acquainted with some good men and women on the way, and I believe I am still welcome in their houses.

Clayton has come to believe that the Lord guided his hand when he shot me, punishing me in that way for my lie, and at the same time saving me from serious harm. He has now decided to study French and divinity both, and then preach in Paris, France. "They're all foreigners there," he says, "but at least they stay in one place and you don't have to chase after them." He writes long letters to me all the time, partly because he and Clemmy have had a parting of the ways, but mostly because our journey together made us more friendly. Clemmy is now being courted by a man who makes drawings of trestles and grade crossings for the Missouri Central Railroad.

Naturally, I do not know what Hanna is doing. I have dreamed of her twice since June. In my first dream, which I dreamed in July, I was walking through the woods up in Canada and more or less accidentally met her coming the other way. "Hello, cousin," she said, and I said hello back, and we both just walked past each other. In my second dream, which I dreamed last month, she was walking through the same woods with Caroline Burke and Aunt Eusie. They were all three wearing white dresses, like they were on their way to a party, and they smiled as they went by, and after they got out of sight one of them started to giggle. In this second dream I rode up to Canada on a mule I rented from Mr. Pewbrace for a dollar and a half a week.

Of course, it is not likely that I will ever see her again. However, it is possible. Whether I do, or whether I do not, I will never forget her or the road that took me to her. I met her because I told some lies, and telling lies is wrong. Still, I cannot say I am sorry I told them, because that would not be true.